His mother loos[...]d mo[...] cheeks. Her fingers were [...] through [...].

"I was so frightened . . . so frightened."

Robert's dad put his hand on her shoulder, dwarfing it. He said, "Your brother is missing."

Robert nodded. "I know."

"How do you know? Did the Mounties tell you?" his father asked.

"No." Robert wanted to close his eyes, to get away from all this, because he didn't understand what was happening. But somewhere inside he had known about this disappearance the moment the blood egg had broken. Maybe even when he'd heard the truck passing his house. "I . . . I think I guessed."

# DUST

### ARTHUR SLADE

LAUREL-LEAF
BOOKS

Published by
Dell Laurel-Leaf
an imprint of
Random House Children's Books
a division of Random House, Inc.
New York

Visit us on the Web! www.randomhouse.com/teens

Educators and librarians, for a variety of teaching tools, visit us at www.randomhouse.com/teachers

ISBN: 0-440-22976-6

RL: 6.0

Reprinted by arrangement with Wendy Lamb Books

Printed in the United States of America

October 2004

10 9 8 7 6 5 4 3 2 1

OPM

For

W. O. Mitchell,

Wallace Stegner,

and Ray Bradbury

I want to sincerely thank: Scott Treimel, my agent, for arriving at the perfect time. Marie Campbell, for taking on this project and helping me find the magic in the story. Wendy Lamb, for her insight. And my wife, Brenda Baker, for her love (and her editing skills).

I also gratefully acknowledge the financial assistance of the Saskatchewan Arts Board and the Canada Council. For anyone who would like to know more about my writing, please visit www.arthurslade.com. The first chapter of this novel was broadcast on CBC Radio Saskatchewan. For those who wondered what happened next, read on....

# CHAPTER ONE

Matthew Steelgate had five cents in his pocket and a yearning for chewing gum and licorice. He wasn't sure which he wanted more, but he knew he could buy both and have at least a penny left over. He walked along the edge of the grid road, three miles from his family's farm and about two miles from Horshoe. The sky was cloudless.

The sun had shifted nearer to the earth in the past half hour, so near that the air crackled with heat. Matthew, following his mother's bidding, wore a straw hat. Like his father's, his neck was tanned brown, along with his face, hands, and forearms to the line where he rolled up his sleeves. The prairie had marked Matthew as one of its own. He understood the connection between himself and the land, understood that he belonged there; when the wind blew, when the rain dotted his face, when the snow fell, he belonged. When the sun darkened his skin, he knew the invisible rays were also working on the field of wheat beside him.

He patted his shirt pocket and was rewarded with a muffled clinking. He had spent three weeks saving this cache of coins, payment for helping his older brother, Robert, with chores. Three weeks dreaming about town. About candy.

A daddy longlegs darted out of a crack in the road and

Matthew squashed it underfoot, then examined the flattened body. It looked like a gray flower pressed and dried between pages in a book. Its insides were outside now. A friend had said that killing a spider meant seven days of rain, so Matthew squashed any he could. Next, he crushed a few grasshoppers inching across the road, but he quickly grew bored.

Even though he was tired, he quickened his pace. He had a good head start on his parents, but if he dawdled he'd soon hear the *clop clop* of the horses' hooves and the rattling of chains on the wagon, followed by his father's voice saying, "Hello there, partner. Going our way?"

He hoped to reach town before his parents. That would be an accomplishment. He would stand proudly on the corner of the street, waving as they arrived to pick up nails and tractor parts. He'd shout out, "See, Mom, I made it. My legs *aren't* too short." That'd show her. She had told him to ride in the wagon, but he'd convinced her that he could travel on his own by running three times around the table as fast as he could. He'd only knocked over one chair. His father had laughed. His mother had relented.

A low, distant rumble made him think of thunder. But thunder needed clouds, didn't it? And the sky was clear as glass.

The sound came from behind him. He turned and saw a truck on the horizon, a black, sun-streaked square that wavered in the heat. It vanished into a gully, then appeared again seconds later. He walked into the shallow ditch along the road, wading through the belly-high yellow grass, and watched the truck approach.

A grasshopper, holding tight to a strand of swaying grass, banged its head against Matthew's back, making a small tobacco-spit stain. When the truck neared, the grasshopper leapt into the air, wings clicking.

Matthew didn't recognize the truck. Very few people around Horshoe drove their vehicles; most saved the gas for tractors. The truck looked old, an ancient vehicle from a far-off time, its big knobby tires spinning. The sun flashed across the windshield, making him squint.

He stared at the curved fenders, watched as the steel-spoked wheels turned more and more slowly. The truck stopped, rocked back and forth; the grumbling noise died, and the prairie was silent. No crickets singing. No grasshopper wings whirring. All was still. Matthew breathed in, waiting for a sound. For motion.

Then the door on the other side opened, hinges screeching. In the ditch, Matthew was low enough to see under the truck. A dark boot hit the ground, then another.

A man walked around the front of the vehicle and stopped near the edge of the road. He gazed across the prairie, as though he was just catching a breath of fresh air. He was tall and lean, wearing a long, beige trench coat. His shoulders were a wide crescent. His face, even under the shade of his circular brimmed hat, was pale.

He must be hot, Matthew figured.

The man looked toward the ditch, almost as though his name had been whispered. His eyes were hidden behind round, dark-lensed glasses.

3

"Hello," the stranger said. His voice reminded Matthew of dry leaves rustling across autumn earth. "How are you today, young man?"

"Good," Matthew answered.

The man smiled. "What's your name?"

"Matthew." Matthew shifted his weight from one foot to the other. He clutched a handful of grass.

"Well, Matt, where are you traveling to?"

"Town."

"Why you going there?"

"To buy gum . . . and . . . and licorice."

The tall man nodded. "Now, that's a very noble pursuit." He ran a finger below his eye as if wiping away a tear. He was wearing black leather gloves. Matthew wondered if his hands were soft. He didn't know anyone who wore gloves during summer. The man smiled again. "Tell me, Matt, have you ever ridden in a truck?"

"Sure, lots of times," Matthew said, nodding.

"Would you like to ride in my truck?"

Matthew let go of the grass. He looked to the east, down a long, straight road. "Mom and Dad are coming along soon," he explained.

The man was silent, as if what Matthew had said required deep thought. "Wouldn't you like to beat them to town? Wouldn't that be nice?"

Matthew narrowed his eyes.

"It would, wouldn't it?" The man's soft voice carried easily across the space between them; it seemed to Matthew that the stranger was whispering right into his ear. "I can see that gum too, Matt. It's on the second shelf in the pool hall candy counter. Red Hand Chewing Gum. It's pink, it's wrapped in waxed paper, and it's in the shape of a cigar. It's waiting for you. Would you like to see it?"

Matthew's tongue explored his moist cheeks. He shifted his weight from side to side.

The man opened the passenger door and gestured. "Your place is here." He paused. "The gum is waiting for you."

Matthew breathed in and walked slowly up the ditch. He stopped on the road, looked in the door.

"Go ahead."

Matthew peered at the dusty seat. He pictured the gum sitting on the shelf, saw himself pointing, saw Mr. Parsons reaching for it. He would get to town so much faster with a ride. He stepped onto the mud rail, then pulled himself into the truck.

The door closed softly.

The stranger was seated on the driver's side. How had he gotten there so quickly? The man sat still momentarily, humming softly and rubbing his chin as though pondering deeply. Then he slid the gearshift down. They rolled smoothly ahead. Matthew couldn't remember him starting the motor.

The man's skin, which showed between his glove and the sleeve of his coat, was the color of the moon. Muscles writhed beneath that ivory layer as the stranger turned the wooden steering wheel and they headed to the middle of the road. The truck accelerated gracefully; weeds became a yellow blur. The engine was a distant hum.

Matthew heard a muffled rattle. He peeked through the oval-shaped back window. A stack of red clay jars, about the same size as his mom's honey pots, were all tied together. They glowed. Or was it the way the sun caught their sides? A pink hair ribbon was trapped under one, flapping. Beside them were several bundles wrapped in burlap. Strips of shiny metal, about six inches wide and six feet long, sat piled on the far side.

"Do you like being young?" the man asked.

Matthew didn't understand the question. He examined the stranger's smiling face. After a moment's thought he answered, "Yes."

"I was never young," the man said. He tipped his hat back, showing glistening white hair. "Do you believe me? I was never young."

Everyone was young at one time—Matthew knew that. His father had once been a little boy and his mother a little girl, and even his grandma had been a kid long before her skin wrinkled and sagged and her teeth fell out. But he also knew that adults understood more about the world than he did, and he trusted in the wisdom of the giants who hovered above him.

"I think I believe you."

The pale man nodded. The windows were rolled up; the cab

grew hot and the air smelled stale. Sweat lined Matthew's fore-head. He looked down at a butterfly husk on the floor below his dangling feet.

They drove on, and over time he grew more comfortable with the stranger. They passed an abandoned farm, the house gray and paintless, windows black like empty eye sockets. The wind had ripped the shingles from the roof. The barn leaned to one side, threatening to collapse. Matthew knew the drought had killed this place. The drought was a monster made of dust—it had dried up the crops so the cows couldn't eat and had driven away the folks who had once lived there. His mom worked hard to keep that same dust out of their house, stuffing rags in the bottom of the door and along the windowsills. Despite her efforts, the grit always found its way into the cupboards, the beds, and their food.

The truck's motor lulled him and time shifted to a slower speed. He watched roads go by, more ghost farms, as though he and the man were traveling in a loop. He pictured the gum again, tried to keep the image in his head.

Then towering grain elevators appeared on the horizon. The rail yard and a collection of houses became visible as the truck cleared an incline.

"What is this town called?" the man asked. Time snapped back to normal speed.

"Horshoe," Matthew answered, scratching at his arm. The man nodded.

They drove past the access road and the stranger studied the town as they went by. Matthew stared too, his heart speeding up. He peeked through the back window as the elevators were eclipsed by a hill.

"Why don't we stop?" Matthew asked.

The man smiled. "Because you're a child. And you know what it's like to be young." He paused. "I was never young. I was never, ever young."

# CHAPTER TWO

**H**E WAS SUPPOSED TO READ THE BIBLE. THE GOOD BOOK. THE ONLY book allowed in their household, except for a hymnal from the Anglican Church and his father's copy of *The Farmer's Almanac*. The Bible was what his mom said he should read.

Instead, Robert was away on Barsoom—not here, in the brown dust of Saskatchewan, but there, in the red dust of the fourth planet from the sun, battling green, manlike, four-armed Tharks. Leading armies into vast citadels with walls of thick purple stone. Fighting with valor, ferocity, and prowess.

I am John Carter, Robert thought. I am the warlord.

The book was *The Warlord of Mars*. He liked it more than *Tarzan of the Apes* or *Treasure Island*. His uncle Alden had slipped it to him on the sly on the last day of school, and Robert had read it several times since then. His uncle had hundreds of books, each one with a magical world inside it.

"Your brother's going to walk to town," his mom yelled up the stairwell.

He snapped the book closed and jammed it beneath the pillow; then he opened the Bible and listened for creaking on the steps. "Did you hear me? Your brother's walking to town. By himself."

Robert thought for a second. She wanted him to go with Matthew, but she wasn't insisting. It wasn't a job, like separating the cream. He had a choice.

He always had to spend time with Matthew. They shared a room, the same toys, even some of the same clothes.

I'm not moving, Robert decided. I want to be alone. He had come up to this hot, stuffy room to get away from them all. To travel to another world. He wished he could be John Carter, who had, with his feet on an Arizona mountainside, fixed the planet Mars in his gaze, closed his eyes, reached out his hand, and been there. Just like that.

"Well?" His mother sounded impatient. Soon she would tell him to go. But Matthew was seven. When I was seven, Robert thought, I walked to town on my own.

"I'm gonna stay here," he announced.

There was a loud, dramatic sigh. *Exasperated,* that was the word he would use to describe that sound. *Exasperated.* He enjoyed all five syllables. Mom was exasperated.

He heard her walk back to the kitchen. Her footsteps didn't clump the way they did when she was mad. At those times her weight seemed to double. Or did her feet turn into big stones?

He read the opening page of the Holy Bible: "Translated out of the original tongues and with the former translations diligently compared and revised, by His Majesty's special command."

He liked the sound of that. It meant the king of Great Britain had ordered his smartest scholars to diligently translate this Bible.

He had issued a *special* command. Had maybe even touched this very book with a royal scepter.

It was too soon after hearing his mother's voice to return to *The Warlord of Mars,* so he flipped ahead in the Old Testament. It listed tribes of the desert with long, strange names. They were always adding and subtracting in the Bible: measuring to build the ark, tallying the names of the wicked people. It was like the math he studied in school. God must enjoy counting, he decided.

The numbers reminded Robert of his brother. He *was* seven, wasn't he? Seven was old enough to do things on your own. Being eleven, Robert had more responsibilities: more chores, more weeding, more pails of water to lug to the barn. And when he was seven, he had walked to town alone.

Or had he been eight?

It didn't matter. He needed to read. He retrieved the book from under his pillow. It was a good story, so full of action. It was Barsoom-hot in his room, and he felt the way the warlord in the Martian desert must have, hot with battle lust, sword burning for blood. He read for a long while, on this other world, this place called Barsoom, far, far away in space and time.

After a while, Robert heard a low drone out on the road. He briefly considered checking which neighbor was going to Horshoe, but he decided to keep reading. Nevertheless, part of his mind was drawn by the sound. He pictured a truck; he didn't know why. The noise faded. He read until his mother's voice ascended the stairwell.

"Your father and I are going to town now," she said. He stuffed the book under his pillow. "Don't forget to feed the chickens."

"I won't," he answered. His words sounded hollow, echoing in his room. The house already seemed empty. He strained to catch the opening and closing squeak of the front door. Nothing.

Curious, he got off the bed and looked out the window into the front yard. The wagon was at the end of the entranceway, led by Smokie and Apache, their horses. His parents sat like statues, his dad holding the reins. The wagon disappeared down the road, a small cloud of dust behind it. But Robert couldn't hear them; it was like watching a silent movie. He was alone.

He had waited for this all afternoon. So why did he feel so . . . so ill at ease? So anxious? *Apprehensive.* He looked at the distant, rolling lines of the Cypress Hills. He wished he could see toward Horshoe.

Maybe he'd feel better if he went outside. Sometimes being in the open helped shift his mind into that special dreaming place. He would imagine the people who had walked this land many years ago: the Indians and the explorers and the North-West Mounted Police in their crimson uniforms, gun barrels glinting, all in a line on their steeds, hooves leaving deep impressions as they galloped across the hills.

He stashed *The Warlord of Mars* under his bed and set the Bible on the desk. Then he crept down the stairs, holding the banister. Each step creaked and cracked.

Everyone was gone, but Robert sensed a presence. At the

landing he peered around the corner, saw nothing but the kitchen table, the tall red vase by the window, and a cloth flour bag on the counter. The De Laval cream separator, with all its bowls and pipes, loomed on the cupboard like a Martian instrument of torture.

He walked toward the front door. Why did he still feel apprehensive? This was his free time. No parents. No Matthew. Just worlds magically unfolding out of his imagination.

He stopped to look at the oval framed photograph on the mantel of his uncle Edmund in uniform. Uncle Edmund looked like Robert's mother, his face thin, eyes sunken. Robert had never met him, but he knew his uncle had been very brave. In 1914 an archduke had been killed and the British had declared war on the Germans. And England was like Canada's big brother, so Edmund and thousands of Canadian soldiers signed up to fight the Great War in Europe, a war so big it had ended all wars. Robert could picture them lining up across the whole country, getting on trains, climbing into ships, and landing in France. Edmund had been shot during a charge over the trenches in the battle for Vimy Ridge. The bullet had struck him right in the heart. He had given his life for a cause, died a hero. Robert often concocted stories about his uncle taking out machine gun nests, or going over the trench to rescue a wounded comrade. Robert had even dreamed about him several times.

Long ago, in one of his games, Robert had decided that it was good luck to touch the photograph. Rarely did he pass it without pressing his fingers to the glass. I'll feel better if I touch it, he told himself. He reached out his hand, fingers spread, and tapped his uncle's shoulder.

Uncle Edmund blinked.

Robert jerked his hand away, eyes wide with shock. His uncle stared back then, with calm, unblinking eyes. Robert was seeing things. That was all. It was the same old picture.

He went outside. Heat thickened the air. The slender hairs on his neck slowly stood on end. It was that familiar electrical current that preceded a storm, but there were no signs in the sky. Just a vacant, bleached blue color. And yet the feeling was there. That "something is going to happen" feeling. Soon.

Robert walked toward the barn that his father had built in a time when he'd talked about wheat as tall as sunflowers and cattle as heavy as hippopotamuses. In the past five years the wind-driven dust had peeled the paint and aged the building. It tilted west.

It was still a sturdy home for Cerberus. When they'd bought the milk cow, his father had let Robert name her. But when his mother had asked who Cerberus was, and Robert had explained that this was the name of the dog who guarded Hell's gate, she'd become furious and insisted they change the cow's name to Dot.

Robert still called her Cerberus, and she answered to it anyway.

Inside the barn the familiar smells of dried manure and old straw filled his nostrils. Robert believed there was magic here, because this was where the calves were pushed out of their mothers, heads or tails first, bodies wrapped in gooey sacs. The calves' first bawling cries had consecrated this place (there was another word he liked), had made it so the wind never worked its way inside.

Three kittens—one gray, one black, and one calico—padded out to greet him. He patted each in turn, then walked to the feed room. He lifted the latch and opened the door, the light widening across the pile of oats. A soft scurrying followed. The kittens darted in and hunted around, but failed to catch any of the mice that had been cavorting in the grain.

He scooped half a pail of chicken feed out of a sack in the corner, then headed to the coop, a small red structure that looked like a sawed-off outhouse.

None of the chickens was outside. They usually spent their time pecking at the ground, gobbling up anything that would fit in their beaks, which would eventually come out their other ends in white and gray piles that they'd leave around the yard like splashes of paint. Today they were hiding.

Robert poured the chicken feed into the small wooden trough, not worrying about spilling it, since the birds didn't care whether they ate off the ground. If his father had been here, he would have given Robert a talking-to for that. "Keep your mind on your job," his dad always grumbled. His dad and Matthew were good at carrying pails. It was hard, Robert thought, to concentrate on something so simple. So . . . mundane? Was that the right word?

Robert spilled a little more, causing a tiny chicken-feed avalanche. Then he walked to the door of the coop. The slim twine that usually held the door shut was broken. He peered inside at the beds of straw. No chickens. He tied the door open using the remainder of the twine. His head brushed the top of the door frame.

"Here chicky-chick-chicks," he said, taking a few steps. The chickens were huddled in a corner, backs against the farthest wall, looking like a dirty snowbank partly buried in the straw. They shook.

He picked up the nearest hen. She cowered but didn't struggle. She seemed petrified.

"Your food is outside." He set the chicken down. "It's in the trough."

His voice echoed as if he were in a cave. The chickens didn't move. Robert searched their roosts for eggs but couldn't find any.

He finally lifted the hens one by one and discovered three eggs. They were an odd gray color, and heavy. He placed them gently in the pail. Nothing felt right about this day anymore.

He put the pail back in the feed room; then, holding the eggs against his chest with his left hand, he used his right to lock the door. He had to give a good push, and one of the eggs slipped from his grip.

It dropped slowly through the air, spinning like a planet in space. It smashed against the hard dirt, spreading a red gunk across the ground.

Blood eggs. Robert had seen one a few years ago. They were eggs that had somehow gone bad, his dad had explained, and instead of yolk and the white stuff, everything inside was a red sticky gunk.

The cats wouldn't go near it.

He felt the odd weight of the other two eggs. He didn't like the look of them. They were probably the same. You couldn't cook them, and if he took them back home and his mom broke them, she might think the Devil had wormed his way into the house. Robert hid them beneath a pile of old straw.

As he stood up he heard a motor rev outside. Two doors slammed shut.

A man yelled, "Hello, anyone home?"

# CHAPTER THREE

**R**OBERT PEERED INTO THE FARMYARD. TWO MEN WERE AT THE FRONT door of his house, the bigger one banging away with a ham-sized fist. They were dressed in dark blue uniforms, high brown boots, and Stetsons. Their pants had a yellow Cavalry stripe running down each leg. A Royal Canadian Mounted Police car sat behind them.

They were majestic in their movements, like knights trying to enter a castle. Many years ago, men like these two had built Fort Walsh in the hills, after all those Indians had been massacred by wolfers.

Mounties. Standing right here. He bet they were from the detachment in Gull Lake.

One man opened the door. He took half a step inside, then paused, as though he'd heard a noise.

He knows I'm watching, Robert thought. He ducked back into the barn and sat silent for a few moments. His heartbeat quickened. He took a breath, then slowly peeked around the corner.

The Mountie was staring straight at him.

"Hello!" the man yelled. He closed the door and strode

toward the barn, his long legs quickly covering yards of ground. The other officer followed, glancing around as if expecting trouble. "Are you Robert Steelgate?"

Robert's lips were frozen. All he had to do was spit out a yes, but shyness had formed a stone on his tongue.

"Is that your name, son?" The Mountie was only a few feet away. His footsteps seemed to shake the earth. "Is that you?"

"Yes," Robert mumbled. "Yes, that's me. I'm Robert Steelgate."

He studied the Mountie. The man looked as though he had been carved from solid stone, then had life breathed into him by a cruel-mouthed god. But his eyes were kind.

"My name is Sergeant Ramsden, and this is Officer Davies. I . . ." It was strange that this man would hesitate. His every word should have been forceful and confident. And yet, he had paused. "I . . . Your parents phoned and asked us to bring you into town."

"Why?"

"Because something has happened, and you should be with your mom and dad," the sergeant answered. He surveyed the farmyard; then his piercing gaze returned to Robert. "Are you ready to go? Is there anything you need?"

What did he need? The question seemed odd. It wasn't going to be a long trip, was it?

"I don't need anything. I guess I'll come along. I have to, don't I?"

Ramsden nodded and started back toward the car. Robert

followed, his eyes drawn to the holster on the sergeant's hip. That's a .455-caliber Colt revolver, Robert thought. He knew the cops used .455s because Jonathan Fawkes, an older kid, had told him so, bragging that he'd once fired one and hit a tin can.

Officer Davies opened the door and Robert slipped into the backseat. Both Mounties removed their hats and sat in front. The silent one drove. They headed west.

Sergeant Ramsden faced Robert, looking over the seat. "Did anyone stop by while your parents were gone?"

"No." Robert thought for a second. He knew that the Mounties needed to know all the details. It was their job. "The chickens seemed scared," he added.

The sergeant furrowed his heavy brow. "What do you mean?"

"They were all huddled together like they thought there was a fox outside, but there wasn't."

"Do you know why they were like that?"

Robert shook his head.

"Did you see any strange vehicles?"

"No. But I did hear one—a truck passed while I was reading."

Ramsden leaned closer. He had a scar that drew a white line from his bottom lip to his chin. Robert wondered if it had been sliced by a knife; maybe the sergeant had fought with a bank robber. Robert imagined two bandanna-wearing men robbing the Broadfoot Trust Company in Gull Lake, then stopping outside to rub their hands in glee and count their loot. The sergeant and his partner would have swept down on them, revolvers blazing, bullets pinging off the car. The bad guys would have surrendered, only to pull a knife when the Mounties holstered their guns.

"Do you know what time you heard the truck?" the sergeant barked.

Robert blinked and shook his head. "After my brother went to town and before my parents left. I was in my room. . . ." A sadness flickered in the sergeant's eyes at the mention of Matthew. "Is my brother all right?"

"What makes you ask that?"

There it was again, a softness behind the eyes, and then stone. "I . . . I just wondered. It seems . . ." It was obvious something had happened. "Is that why you're here?"

"Your parents will answer all your questions." The sergeant cleared his throat. "So you didn't see this truck?"

"No. I was . . . lying down."

"How do you know it was a truck?"

Robert paused. How *did* he know? The sound had been deep and rumbling, and as it passed he had pictured an old truck, dust trailing behind it. He lifted his eyes to the officer. "It was just a feeling I had. . . ." His voice trailed off.

Sergeant Ramsden stared hard at him, then turned to face forward, rubbing a thick hand across his closely cropped hair.

That hand knows jujitsu, Robert thought. He'd once read a flyer that said "Join the Mounties, live the adventure." It listed all the things trainees would learn: musketry, revolver fire, fingerprinting, photography, horseback riding, boxing, map reading, and postmortem examinations. All that information and training was jammed inside these two men. They could handle any situation.

They were halfway to Horshoe already, passing field after field. The hot sun seared the top of the car, so Officer Davies pulled the visor down to block the light. Robert gawked around the interior but couldn't see any bullet holes. He decided that police cars were probably bulletproof.

Both Mounties spent a lot of time searching the prairie. What were they looking for? The world through the window was bleached to whiteness.

Robert was suddenly gripped with a need to look at the roadside ditch, though he wasn't sure what he expected to see. A lump rose in his throat. They went by a place where the grass was partly trampled down. A bad thing had happened there. He was sure of it. He wondered if he should open his mouth to tell them. But what would he say?

The apprehension grew in his stomach. Sweat trickled down his forehead. The air seemed stuffy, even though the driver's window was open. He felt trapped.

He thought of Barsoom. John Carter had flown through the Martian air in a one-man aircraft. Robert sat farther back in his seat so he could see only sky out the window. It made it easier to believe they were flying through the air in a Mountie scout ship.

Suddenly Horshoe's grain elevators rose up like the citadel towers on Barsoom. He wished they were made of stone. Soon the Pioneer and Ogilvie emblems became clear.

The car didn't slow down. Robert swallowed. They seemed to be going past town. A second later the Mountie jammed his foot on the brake and cranked the wheel.

The doubt wouldn't go away; it got darker, bigger. There was something Robert should be afraid of right now, but he wasn't sure what.

Finally, it came to him. He cleared his throat and said, "Seven is too young to walk to town by yourself."

# CHAPTER FOUR

NEITHER MOUNTIE ANSWERED ROBERT, THOUGH THE SERGEANT glanced his way. They drove around the corner onto Main Street. On one side was Harper's Hotel, a two-story building with a false front. A laundry had been attached to the wall facing the alley. The grocery store and the pool parlor were across the street. The Royal Theatre stood alone at the end of the block, its doors nailed shut.

A crowd had gathered in front of the hotel. Robert spotted his family's wagon but not his mom and dad. The Mountie parked the car, and the people were magnetically drawn toward it. The sergeant got out, opened the back door for Robert, and helped him down.

"Where is Mr. Steelgate?" the sergeant asked.

The crowd parted and there stood Robert's parents, unmoving, as though they'd been turned to stone. His father was a tall, wiry man with his sleeves rolled up, his face prematurely wrinkled by the sun and from squinting to keep out the dust. His eyes were red-rimmed, tired. Robert's mother was also tall, her body a frail vessel for her spirit, her clothing plain gray. They looked to be in a trance.

The sergeant spoke their names, breaking the spell. They shuffled like zombies toward Robert. He was frightened by their slowness.

He spotted Uncle Alden standing behind them, thin as a post, one hand lifted up as though he was about to wave hello. Then Robert's mother wrapped her long arms around her son, squeezing him against her bony chest, slender fingers clutching his head. "You stupid, stupid boy." He had never heard her voice so soft. "You're safe. Dear God, you're safe."

Robert was confused. Why was he stupid, and what did she mean by *safe*? He didn't feel safe. He felt as though there were invisible strings pulling at him, and soon one would drag him away.

His mother loosened her grip and moved her hands to his cheeks. Her fingers were cool. She shook as if a chill had run through her. "I was so frightened . . . so frightened."

Robert's dad put his hand on her shoulder, dwarfing it. He said, "Your brother is missing."

Robert nodded. "I know."

"How do you know? Did the Mounties tell you?" his father asked.

"No." Robert wanted to close his eyes, to get away from all this, because he didn't understand what was happening. But somewhere inside he had known about this disappearance the moment the blood egg had broken. Maybe even when he'd heard the truck passing his house. "I . . . I think I guessed."

His mom let go and they stared at him quizzically. Robert had the sick, guilty feeling he had given the wrong answer.

Uncle Alden squeezed Robert's arm. "Don't worry. It's all gonna work out. We'll find your brother. That's why the Mounties and all these people are here."

His uncle looked very serious—grave, in fact. Robert wished this were a different day. If it had been, he could have asked Uncle Alden about Barsoom. About the warlord and the battles with the Tharks. Instead of feeling frightened.

"Your son said he heard a truck go by your house before you left for town," the sergeant said.

"Truck?" said Robert's dad. "I didn't hear a truck go by. Are you sure, son?"

Was he sure? Every question spun webs of doubt around him.

"Are you sure?" his dad repeated quietly.

Robert nodded.

His mother stepped back so she could look down at him. "Why didn't you say something? Why didn't you tell us?"

Robert blinked. "It was just a truck going by. That's all."

Sergeant Ramsden cleared his throat. "Look, there might have been a truck, there might not. The point is, your boy's probably wandering around somewhere daydreaming."

"It's not in Matthew to daydream," Robert's mom said defensively.

The sergeant frowned. He moved toward the sidewalk and spoke to the crowd, who were waiting a respectful distance from the family.

"Listen up. Anyone who's got a truck or a wagon, I need help finding this boy, Matthew. You all know what he looks like. He may have been picked up by someone, so if you see anything odd, wait for us. Don't go getting into any hysterics or heroics—I don't want neither. If you find the boy, bring him right back here."

The crowd slowly dispersed, except for Mrs. Juskin and Mrs. Torence, the two plump war widows who lived in the house next to the school. They had wormed into place beside Robert's mother, intoning quietly that "everything—every single thing" would be all right. The shape of their bodies reminded Robert of a spider's abdomen. Mrs. Torence set her hand on his head. It felt heavy and hot and sweaty like an African toad.

The sergeant asked Robert's uncle, "Do you mind if Officer Davies rides in your truck?"

"I'll go get it," Uncle Alden replied. "Anything to help." He squeezed Robert's arm again, then jogged to his truck. Robert's mom and dad stared silently. They'd become statues again.

The Mounties stepped away to talk privately. Robert watched Sergeant Ramsden's lips move. Officer Davies stood straight, leaning slightly ahead. Occasionally he nodded or said something that could have been *Yes, sir.* The words of his superior officer flowed out and the younger Mountie took them in as though he were a receptacle—there was another good word—to be filled with orders. Maybe the sergeant had given a *special* command. A royal one.

Uncle Alden's old Ford truck rattled and hummed up the street and stopped near the sidewalk. Then Davies got in and spoke a few words. Robert wanted to slip through the open door and go with them, but the moment he had the thought, the door closed and the truck sped off.

Sergeant Ramsden returned. "You three will ride with me."

"You're not taking the boy, are you?" Mrs. Torence asked. "We'll watch over him until you get back." Her hand squirmed on Robert's head and pushed him down as if he were a potato she was trying to plant. "The sandhills and the sage are no place for him."

"The boy comes." Sergeant Ramsden didn't even look at her. "He's got good eyes and ears. And intuition."

Mrs. Torence reluctantly removed her hand, and Robert felt lighter.

"You take care, now, Robbie," one of the widows whispered.

Robert followed his mother, climbing into the backseat of the Mounties' car. His father and the sergeant sat in the front.

He tried hard to remember exactly what *intuition* meant.

# CHAPTER FIVE

**T**HEY DROVE DOWN MAIN STREET. THREE CHINESE WOMEN STOOD outside the laundry, wiping their hands on their aprons, staring into the Mounties' car. Their long black hair was braided and tied back. A wisp of steam drifted out the door behind them. Somewhere inside, the men were boiling water, turning handles on the pressing machine, squeezing the stains from clothes. The women seemed sad, Robert thought. They came from an old country, didn't they? A land of emperors and dragons. People disappeared there all the time, stolen by sinister men like Dr. Fu Manchu. These women would know what it was like to lose someone dear.

"Did your son have any special hiding places?" the sergeant asked as they stopped at the edge of the grid road. "The kind of place he might run to if he were afraid?"

Robert thought the question wasn't very useful. If Matthew had a hiding place, he wouldn't have told anyone; hiding places were secret.

"Can't say I ever saw Matthew frightened," Robert's dad said.

"Is there anywhere he would have gone? An old granary? A potato cellar? If someone had scared him, that is."

"Who would scare him?" Robert's father asked angrily. "Is there something we should know? I'd appreciate the truth."

"Yesterday, a girl went missing in Moose Jaw," the sergeant said slowly. "She was four years old."

Robert's mom moaned in the back of her throat, a trapped sound from deep in a tunnel.

"The detachment there doesn't have any leads," the sergeant continued, "other than someone who says he saw a truck. . . ." He paused. "Look, whoever took that girl—if anyone did—probably wouldn't come this way. They'd go south and cross the border, not west, where every stranger sticks out like a sore thumb. It wouldn't make sense."

"A fellow who steals kids probably isn't in the habit of making sense," said Robert's dad.

A long silence followed. Robert's father cleared his throat, seemed about to ask a question, but didn't.

The sergeant turned to the backseat. Robert was mesmerized by the movement of the muscles in the Mountie's neck, the little bumps of the spine, right below his hairline.

"Do you have any idea where your brother might have gone?"

Robert breathed in. Again, a weight pressed on his tongue. He closed his eyes and saw the image of a truck going west, dust trailing behind it. "West," he answered dreamily. He opened his eyes, squinted. The sun seemed brighter. He glanced from the sergeant's face to his father, who stared as though Robert had spoken in tongues. He quickly added: "Maybe Matthew walked past town. Maybe he did."

Ramsden nodded. He steered the car onto the main road.

Robert was glad he'd chosen to speak up, because he knew west was the right way to go, as a compass knows where to point. He had an inexplicable urge to look through the back window at the grain elevators.

He glanced at his mother. Her eyes were wide open, as if the car were driving through a snowstorm and she didn't dare lose track of the road. She had grown thinner in the past few minutes, the skin tight against her cheekbones. Her lips moved: *"Deargodjesus I pray theealmightysweetlord find us and find our son and hold us close."*

The road led to Maple Creek. Robert had been on it a few times, most recently the previous fall, when his dad had taken him to the cattle sale. But it was essentially a new, unfamiliar road, straight as a railroad track for a mile or so, then twisting and weaving around some hills. They were nowhere near the majestic stature of the Cypress Hills, but they were high enough that things were hidden.

"The unexpected" could happen here, and that was often bad, like a sneaky bandit attack in a western novel.

But it worked the opposite way too. The unexpected could be swell: a grand surprise. Like finding a treasure chest overflowing with gold coins in your backyard, or sitting in your white tent in the middle of the Sahara and having an old friend pop in and say, "Hello, partner."

Robert held his head high to see over the seat. Banks of dirt filled the ditch, and tumbleweeds—Russian thistles, his dad called them—clung to the fence. Had they actually blown in all the way from Russia? He pictured the thistles tumbling over the North Pole and the Yukon and landing here in Saskatchewan. The thistles struggled against the barrier like soldiers trying to scramble over barbed wire. It reminded Robert of how his uncle Edmund had gone over the trenches into no-man's-land.

A brave lad. Uncle Alden had always said his younger brother was a brave, brave lad. They'd fought side by side in France.

The car rounded a corner. Before them, the land was even flatter, the road stretching for miles. Robert's dad craned his neck, leaned ahead, blocking Robert's view.

"He couldn't have walked this far," the sergeant muttered, pressing the brakes.

Robert felt his mom tug on his shirt as she said, "Sit down and let the men do the looking."

He leaned away so that her frail hand fell to the seat; then he stared back out the window.

They reached an approach that led into the sandhills. The sergeant turned the car onto an old trail and asked, "Do you see tracks?"

Robert gripped the edge of the seat to keep from sliding

down when they hit a bump. He saw two lines in the sand. Fresh tire tracks.

The sergeant turned down the approach and followed the trail. Soon the grass became sparse and the bushes short and leafless, as though they didn't want to get too close to the sun. The wind had torn open the tops of the hills, exposing sand. It reminded Robert of Moses and the pharaoh and how God had turned Moses' staff into a snake. First the plague of frogs. Then the locusts. Then the wrath of God. That was the order in the Bible. And long before all of that was the flood. But here, under the wide blue skies, the wind was the flood. Everyone drowned in it.

He thought of Matthew alone on that road, the wind swirling around, lifting him into the air, taking him away. It felt as if that were what had happened.

The road lost definition, but they could still make out the tire tracks, obscured slightly by drifting sand. The sergeant inched the vehicle ahead.

Robert wondered if the sand would continue to spread the way the ice once had thousands of years ago, slowly taking over the soil. A sand age. Or the way the cancer had spread through the old milk cow's eye and into her brain, killing her.

Suddenly, the car stopped.

The sergeant craned his neck and squinted. "Hmmm. The tracks end, just like that." He used the steering wheel to pull himself up and get closer to the windshield.

"To the right, go . . . go there," a voice said. Robert gawked around for the source, but then noticed everyone was looking at him. Had he said it?

"What was that?" the sergeant asked.

Robert kept his mouth shut.

The sergeant's eyes were soft again. He clunked the car into gear and steered right. Moments later he again found the tracks, which ran between two low hills.

Robert swallowed. His stomach churned, as if there were worms wriggling through it. Was this *apprehension* again? He saw a brown, ancient truck. Sun glinted off the chrome, blinding him. A shadow moved beside it; then the truck vanished.

His head ached, and he knew somehow, in his gut, that he'd seen the past. Matthew's past.

A semicircular ridge of hills provided little protection from the wind. The tracks ended again and the sergeant stopped the car. He lifted his hat, rubbed at his bristly hair.

"Mr. Steelgate, please come with me," the sergeant said as he got out, the door squeaking in protest. Robert's dad pushed open his own door, sand grinding in its hinges. The wind whistled in, playing a soft note. Then they shoved the doors closed, silencing the song.

His mother moaned and rocked herself back and forth, her lips slightly parted, her eyes dull.

"Nooohhh."

He grasped her hand and she closed her eyes, lowered her voice, and began humming a soft hymn. He recognized it from church.

The sergeant and Robert's dad crept into the gully. Ramsden examined an object on the ground. Tire tracks? Robert pulled himself up higher, keeping one hand on his mother's. No, it was a red clay jar about six inches high. It looked broken.

He felt the need to touch it. He let go of his mom and yanked on the door handle.

"Noooohhh," she moaned more loudly.

He swallowed and quietly said, "Sorry, I have to go." He pushed open the door and a squadron of grasshoppers leapt away. They were here, too, even though the grass was mostly dead. Their dark eyes were so much larger than the rest of their heads, like little black pearls. They hopped skyward as he walked.

His mother's moaning became softer with each step. The object was indeed a broken jar. There was a dried orange residue on the inside. The jar looked as though it had come out of a pharaoh's tomb, with images that seemed like drawings and writing at the same time on the side. Hieroglyphs—he'd read about them in a book lent to him by his uncle.

Robert touched the orange substance.

*"I've lost my doll."* A girl's sad voice echoed inside Robert's head. *"I've lost my doll. Will you find it for me?"* He leaned closer to the jar, rubbed inside. Nothing.

He watched as Ramsden searched a clump of half-grown bushes. The sergeant reached for something hanging in the barbed branches, pulled it out as though he were performing a magic trick. Robert's dad staggered back.

It was Matthew's straw hat.

# CHAPTER SIX

**F**OUR WEEKS LATER, ROBERT WAS STANDING ON THE TRAIN TRACKS next to the Pioneer grain elevator. The tracks stretched in a long line from his feet to forever. They looked like the spine of a dead dinosaur or giant sea snake. What were the backbones called again? *Vertebrae*. That was the word scientists used. *Archae-ologists*—the guys who dug in dirt, who had found Tutankhamen buried in Egypt—would say these were *vertebrae*. Snake verte-brae.

It would have had to be a giant snake, though, like the one that wrapped itself around the world in the Viking legends. But that serpent was under the ocean. Maybe Saskatchewan had been underwater once too. And the sun had shone and shone and dried up everything, including the snake, leaving just its bleached bones.

"Robert." His dad's voice cut through his thoughts. "Get over here."

Robert jogged toward the elevator. His father had finished dealing with the agent and now sat on the wagon, his jaw set hard. It had been set hard for quite a while now.

Robert climbed to his seat. His dad flicked the reins and the horses trotted down the road, their iron horseshoes *ping ping*ing as they crossed the tracks.

Main Street was almost empty; a truck sat in front of the grocer's and a wagon stood by the hotel. Robert had to count silently to figure out what day it was. Saturday. He wanted to buy candy at Mr. Parsons's Billiards and Barber Shop, but he had no pennies and didn't feel brave enough to ask for any.

His father parked near the grocer's and swung to the ground. "I'll be back in twenty minutes," he said; then he plodded across the wooden sidewalk.

Old Mr. Gundy sat on the bench outside the store, whittling a piece of wood. He glanced away from Robert's dad. Robert had seen that a lot lately. People didn't look at him or his mom or dad. It was as if they didn't exist anymore. Or maybe no one wanted to see what was in their eyes.

His dad hadn't told him to stay put, so he climbed down and walked to the pool parlor. His mom had forbidden him to go in there, because the men who played pool on the long tables always took the Lord's name in vain. Swearing was a sin, he knew that much. Those ruffians would feel God's wrath, maybe even get hit by lightning while brandishing their pool cues. It'd be quite the sight to see, he decided, so long as God didn't also strike down boys who watched from the sidelines.

A barber's pole, its colors faded, twirled slowly in the window. He pushed on the door; it had been hung crooked, so it slid across a groove in the floor. Cigarette smoke drifted up his nose. The parlor was hazy, giving him the impression the building was quite close to that "hot place" far below. He pictured the Devil lying under the floorboards, blowing smoke between the cracks.

Robert stood in the barbershop, which was separated from the pool parlor by a low railing. The barber's chair was a majestic, long-backed metal seat padded with red leather cushions. When Mr. Parsons cut hair he'd swivel it around so his clients could watch the games. Uncle Alden had paid for Robert to have his hair cut in that very throne. It was the grandest haircut he'd ever had. The chair smelled of hair oils and dried shaving foam. A washbasin sat on the counter, surrounded by bottles of blue and red oils.

He turned to the glass candy counter. An intricate brass cash register rested on top. Lined up behind the smudged glass were all the things he could have bought if only he'd had a few pennies. Chocolate wafers, Red Hand Chewing Gum, licorice, jawbreakers, and small sugar candies that were ten for a penny. His mouth watered. He tried to commit them to memory.

A sharp *crack* drew his attention toward the pool room. The unshaven men at the long tables were dressed in dirty work clothes, hand-rolled cigarettes dangling from their lips. A few were out-of-towners, maybe even hobos on their way east or west, trying to outrun the drought.

They glanced at him with a flick of the head, no more. It was as though a bird of ill omen were perched on his shoulder, invisible to him. If they looked too long they might miss their shots, lose their good luck.

In an attempt to be less conspicuous, he leaned against the door frame and watched as colors swirled around the tables. Each ball became a planet and the players gods, moving entire worlds.

Mike Tuppence, a boy of six or seven, sat on a chair in the corner. He wore suspenders and an oversized shirt that might have belonged to an older brother. His family lived way up on the bench, the tallest part of the Cypress Hills. Robert's mom had once said she pitied Mike because his mother had died giving birth to him. The doctor had pulled hard to get little Mike into this world, and now Mike was being dragged through all the sinful places in Horshoe and had no chance of growing up straight. It didn't help that his father was a drinker.

Mike saw Robert. He got down from his chair one foot at a time and arched his back like a cat. He shuffled over, then leaned against the other side of the door frame, exploring his teeth with a toothpick, eyes focused on the game.

Robert glanced down. Mike's feet were bare and horribly dirty.

Mike took the toothpick out of his mouth. "They're gonna open the movie parlor again," he said.

"Oh?"

"Yeah, that new guy's gonna do it, and he'll play a film. Dad said he'd take me."

Robert had seen several talkies and a couple of five-cent silent films with Uncle Alden. When his mom found out, she'd spanked Robert with the wooden spoon and yelled at his uncle, swearing he'd only be allowed to visit at Christmas and Easter. She'd relented a month or so later, but she kept the spoon hanging on a nail in the kitchen as a reminder to Robert.

"It should be fun," Mike said.

A man cursed when his ball bounced out of a pocket. Robert looked up, expecting lightning. Nothing happened. God must be busy today, he decided. Or maybe he's out of lightning bolts.

"So's Matthew coming to town?" Mike asked.

Robert thought hard about the question. "No," he said finally. "He can't."

"Why not? Did he do something bad?"

"No."

"When will he come?"

"He can't come. He's gone."

Mike watched his father hit the cue ball and miss his target. Another curse was launched into the room and it hung in the air.

"I know he's gone away, Dad said so. But he's gonna come back, isn't he? So's we can play together?"

Robert glowered at him. "He's not coming back. Not ever. He's probably dead, okay? Dead. Like a little sparrow that falls out of the nest. Dead."

The word had a weight all its own, could be swung like a hammer. Robert still didn't know exactly what it meant.

Mike looked up at Robert, disbelieving, eyes welling up with tears. He slumped his shoulders and went back to his chair.

Robert felt sick in his gut and angry. He wished he hadn't used that word. He walked out of the hall and across the wooden sidewalk. The sun forced him to squint. He climbed into the wagon and waited for his father.

He wondered about what he had just said. Matthew had been gone for more than four weeks, and that was a very long time. Four weeks was two fortnights, and that equaled a month. If Matthew had been trapped in a hole somewhere, by now he would have died from thirst, or starved. His parents hadn't talked about Matthew's disappearance since those first two weeks of frantic searching. And the Mounties had lost the trail. That didn't make sense to Robert, because they were always supposed to get the bad guy. There was talk that a man had taken Matthew, but no proof of it. Two new people had moved to Horshoe, but neither seemed to be involved.

Robert liked to think that Matthew had gotten sick and been adopted by a momma coyote. She would have dragged him to her den, stuffing him with wild onions and rabbits. Matthew would return in the fall knowing how to howl like a coyote and hide in gullies.

Last week, Robert had overheard Mr. Ruggles say, "That Steelgate kid is dead, I bet, dried up to bones in the hills." The grocer had looked over his shoulder, seen Robert, and silently walked to the back room, out of shame, or fear of being infected by disease.

Dead. Robert tried to understand the word. If Matthew was dead, then had he really gone to Heaven, to the very place their mom always talked about? He thought of the calves that had died that spring—were they up there too?

"You daydreaming again, Robert?" A soft voice startled him. Uncle Alden stood next to the wagon, head cocked to one side. His green eyes glittered with humor. He looked a lot like Robert's mom, with the same gaunt, slightly haunting features, as though they had both experienced a frightening event in their youth. But if there'd been such an event, then his uncle, at least, had learned to smile since that day.

"You on Barsoom? Or in Neverland?"

Robert blinked. "No. Just thinking about Matthew."

Uncle Alden nodded sagely. "Yeah. There's a lot to think about, isn't there? I really wish I knew where he's gone. I'm worried about your parents, too. How has your mom been?"

"Sad," Robert said. It was the only word that expressed everything. "Really sad. She doesn't move much, only to cook. Then she sits in the rocking chair and stares out the window."

"It's tough. Your mom—she changed a lot when Edmund died and it still weighs heavy on her. She prays harder now, maybe even too hard, but she wants to keep us all safe."

Robert nodded. His mom was always praying: when they got up, before they ate, before they went to bed. Even sometimes in front of Uncle Edmund's picture, with tears in her eyes. It was as though she hoped the prayers would cast a protective spell around the family.

"How is your dad?"

"Angry." Robert didn't think he had to explain any further.

"Everyone blames themselves. Wonders what they could have done to change things."

Robert thought about the word *blame*. It was there in the house, on the walls, echoing in the hallways. Blame. Maybe even directed toward him. After all, he *was* the older brother, and he had chosen not to go with Matthew.

"Everything will work out," his uncle promised.

Robert looked up. Uncle Alden glanced away as though he didn't believe what he'd just said.

The door to the grocer's opened and Robert's dad walked out, clutching a cloth sack and a box of nails. He saw his brother-in-law and frowned. "What are you up to, Alden?" he asked gruffly, dropping his purchases in the wagon.

"Waiting for the hail," Uncle Alden answered cheerfully. "It came this time last year."

"Don't even joke about hail. That's the last thing we need."

Uncle Alden shrugged. "Sorry, Garland. Joking is a bad habit I'm trying to break." He paused. "You hear about that guy in Regina?"

"What guy?"

"Went to get a tooth pulled out at the dentist, sat back, opened his mouth, and in jumped a grasshopper. Nearly choked to death. Darnedest thing was, when the grasshopper popped back out, it was holding the tooth!"

Robert's dad shook his head. "You and your tall tales," he growled, but Robert could see that his father's thin lips had almost turned up in a smile.

"Your son believes me." Uncle Alden winked at Robert. "There's another guy up north who saddled a giant grasshopper, got on, and jumped right to the moon."

Robert laughed. His dad shot him a mean look. "Don't you encourage your uncle." This time he was smiling crookedly, as if only half his face knew how. "He's a bad influence."

Uncle Alden grinned. "Need a hand with anything at home?"

"We're fine, thanks. Nothing much to be done right now."

"Call me if anything comes up, and say hi to my sister." Uncle Alden shook Robert's hand, and Robert awkwardly returned the gesture. "See ya, son." His uncle walked away.

Robert's father gave a soft, commanding whistle and flicked the reins. Smokie and Apache snorted, clomping their hooves and backing the wagon onto the street.

Robert watched Uncle Alden get into his truck. He picked something up from the seat and opened it. It looked like a magazine.

Robert wanted to follow him back to his farm south of town. Every time Robert visited he marveled at the books that flowed out of the shelves, how they were piled on the floor and laid open on the kitchen table. More books than the school library. More words than he could read in a lifetime.

# CHAPTER SEVEN

**T**HAT NIGHT, ROBERT SLEPT SOUNDLY FOR THE FIRST TIME SINCE his brother's disappearance, not waking once. He dreamed of Matthew, a gentle dream in which his brother floated outside the second-floor window, shimmering.

Seeing him there seemed as natural as breathing. Matthew rapped at the window, and Robert undid the latch so he could drift into the room. Matthew's eyes were wide and full of joy. He didn't speak, but somehow Robert knew that his brother *had* been living with the coyotes and had gone through a den to another world and seen many wondrous things: talking herons, singing frogs, and a lynx who was king of all the animals. Robert stopped feeling sad. Matthew looked so happy. He hovered there, his lips moving as though he were babbling, which was perhaps the strangest part of the whole dream, since he had always been a quiet boy. He left before the first rays of dawn, making Robert promise not to be glum.

Robert awakened happy and energetic. He slid out of bed and closed the window. Silver dust stained his hands. It sparkled and had an oily nature. He brought his fingers to his nose, sniffed in the scent of wolf willow. It was as though someone had crushed dried wolf willow leaves and strewn the powder across his windowsill. Very odd. He wiped the dust on his pants and noticed that the covers on Matthew's bed were slightly rumpled, just the way they used to be every morning.

It was going to be a grand day. Robert dressed, took the steps two at a time, and dashed outside. His dad was feeding the steers. Robert ran over and grabbed a pail.

"Well, there's no getting out of it, son," Robert's dad said cheerfully, "we're gonna have to go to church today."

Robert carefully poured oats across the hay strewn in the feeding trough.

"Not too much," his dad warned gently, smiling so his teeth showed, "that stuff's like gold."

Robert tipped the pail up a little.

"That's it. Good job."

His father had not spoken so many words to him in ages. Robert felt uneasy hearing them; he wanted more but didn't trust them, because the words might disappear or become angry. He would have to be very careful, do everything exactly as he was told.

When they were finished, his father patted his back, and Robert shuddered slightly. His dad used to pat him on the shoulder and talk about cows as heavy as hippos and wheat as tall as sunflowers. Robert suddenly saw that magical world where everything was bigger. Dragonflies the size of biplanes. Gophers larger than hounds. Giant cow hippopotamuses lumbering around wet fields. No—*hippopotami*!

"I dreamed a wonderful dream last night," his dad murmured, as though it were the biggest secret in the universe. "Everything was growing. I walked out in the wheat field holding your mom's hand, and you and Matthew . . ." He faltered for a moment. "We were all there. It was a good dream. A *real* dream."

A real dream? Robert knew dreams weren't real, but he also knew that some could *become* real.

His dad gave him another pat. They strolled back home.

Inside, his mother greeted them with a grin. During breakfast, his dad touched his mom's hand. They intertwined fingers. Robert nearly dropped his spoon into his porridge.

"It's such a good day," his mother said, "a really good day." She winked at him.

Robert watched with wonder. The moment he was done eating, his mother said, "Why don't you get your fancy duds on, dear? I'll look after the dishes."

Robert nodded, abandoned his bowl, and went upstairs. He put on his best clothes: a pair of black pants, a white button-up shirt that made his skin itch, a bow tie, and black suspenders. Smashing, he thought to himself. I look dapper and smashing. Maybe even gallant. He liked the suspenders the most. They were something grown-ups wore. He strode downstairs, chest puffed out.

Then came a mechanical grunt and growl from outside, followed by a loud *pop!* He rushed out the door. His father was piloting the old roadster up the driveway. It had been stored in the small shed for ages, the favorite bombing target of barn swallows and pigeons, but now it sparkled like new. His father opened the front door for his wife and lifted Robert into the rumble seat.

The car vibrated with life, thrumming under his body. It had been a year since he'd last sat in the car, during a long, bumpy trip to Grandpa Steelgate's funeral in Moose Jaw.

He remembered that day distinctly. He'd come down for breakfast and told his mom that Grandpa Steelgate was dead. He'd known this because he'd had a dream in which Grandpa had danced through a ballroom with an invisible partner, stopped at a door, waved and winked at Robert, then pirouetted through. Robert's mother had told him not to make up things like that. Then a few hours later Mr. Ruggles had brought a telegram announcing Grandpa Steelgate's death. What had followed was a silent, sad trip east.

This trip was not sad, though. It was a new adventure. The air was already sweltering, but a few clouds had scudded out of nowhere, softening the bright sun. The car jerked ahead onto the road; Robert's father laughed and apologized.

His parents seemed to talk excitedly during the trip into town, but out back in the open air, Robert couldn't hear a word. He daydreamed, the sun heating his skin, sweat trickling down the side of his face, cooled by the breeze. The roadster! The name was magnificent. And here he was again in the rumble seat like a dignitary, a duke or a prime minister. Or a royal British prince. He imagined waving to the crowds that waited to get a glimpse of him.

Then they passed that place in the road where the grass had been trampled down. He had once been sure something bad had happened there, but now he wasn't so certain. After all, Matthew had visited him last night and said everything was all right. It was important to believe him.

As the roadster chugged through town, a few people gawked at them. It wasn't that they hadn't seen a car before—many did drive to church—but it was rare to see the Steelgates' car. It made Robert feel special. I'm Prince Robert of Steelgatia, he thought. I'm next in line to the throne. He couldn't help waving. Some girls from school waved back.

His dad parked the roadster near the white picket fence. The church was old and small, perched on a hill with all of Horshoe laid out below it. He wondered if the reverend watched from his rectory to see who came to worship and who didn't. Maybe he even had a big book where he wrote down all the sinners' names. The bell rang, calling the flock. For Robert, the glorious ringing announced his family's arrival. Such an old sound.

They got out of the roadster and walked across the dry grass. The church's stained-glass windows were rounded like the portholes on a ship; a ship in the middle of the prairies, Robert thought. If everyone sang loudly enough, it might sail to Heaven.

Inside, they were hit by thick, warm air. The church was packed, so Robert and his parents sat in a back pew. He preferred that, anyway. He didn't like it when he could feel someone breathe on his neck when they sang.

The pews were worn smooth by bodies sliding down to kneel, getting up to sing. The thick wood had been polished recently, and the smell tingled Robert's nostril hairs. The small chalkboard at the front was emblazoned with three numbers: 40, 23, 136. Each would become a song.

Robert settled himself. Women, and some men, whispered to each other as if to keep God, or the reverend, from hearing their unholy gossip. Everyone was dressed primly and properly; even the Polver family, who Robert knew were poor as beggars, had come in their best patched clothing. Drops of sweat trailed down Mr. Polver's pockmarked face and stains had appeared under his arms. Girls at school said the Polvers ate pig mash with molasses for breakfast, lunch, and supper. Maybe that was why Mr. Polver's teeth were brown.

The last few parishioners came in. *Parishioner*—another word Robert thought he should remember. Someday he would have a grand collection of exciting words.

Reverend Gibbs entered, clad in white robes, with the ends of his long purple sacramental stole flapping. He was heavyset, big in voice and body. People turned forward like rowers in some vast Roman galley, eyes following their drum master. Robert imagined himself heaving and ho-ing to the slow beat of the hymns, striving to reach distant shores.

The reverend boomed words about God blessing the house; then the organ resounded with triumphant chords. The parishioners stood up, clutching their hymnals, and the choir warbled into song. Mrs. Juskin and Mrs. Torence, the two war widows, sat side by side in the choir, mouths wide open, voices blaring. The writing on the chalkboard was extremely neat, with all the proper curls; Mrs. Juskin had probably written down the hymns. She *was* the teacher in town.

Robert's dad nudged him with the hymnal and Robert began to sing. His mom never had to look at the words; she knew them all perfectly.

It was a beautiful hymn about God being a stronghold and a shield. The choir faltered slightly, their clear notes slipping into caterwauling. It made Robert's neck hair stand up. It's a *cacophony*, he thought.

The church door swung open. A well-dressed, slim man sat down in the same row as Robert and his parents. Robert watched him out of the corner of his eye. The man's face seemed to be chiseled from ivory; he held a hat in his hand, and his eyes appeared red. He sang without a book.

Robert tried to get a good look at the stranger. There was no way his eyes could really be red. It had to be a reflection from the stained glass.

His father nudged him again. The choir had found the right key, and the hymn reached its glorious finale. Reverend Gibbs asked everyone to sit down. Robert couldn't help glancing at the newcomer, who looked straight ahead, smiling contentedly.

Mr. Ruggles, the storekeeper, clomped to the front and read from the Bible about drought, and Moses in Egypt, and toads and locusts, and a staff changing into a snake, and the pharaoh, who was a hardened man. It was an amazing story. Robert knew the rest, the way the water parted and Moses and the chosen Israelites walked through it, heading for the promised land. Then the waves crashed together on the Egyptians and their chariots.

It couldn't happen here, Robert decided. There was no ocean, and if it rained frogs they'd get dried up. *Desiccated.* He hadn't seen one since he was seven or eight.

The parishioners prayed and sang and prayed, and finally Reverend Gibbs delivered the sermon. Robert listened, spellbound. The words fit perfectly together. He loved the ring of them, one after the other, built like a temple, filled with understanding. He didn't always comprehend what the reverend spoke about, but he could feel it. There was *meaning* behind these words. And the spirit of God.

The sermon was about animals: the lost sheep of the fold, and the little sparrow that falls out of its nest. God saw them all. Robert knew the reverend was talking about Matthew but not saying his name. He's implying, Robert thought, that's what he's doing. Robert guessed that the parishioners were thinking about Matthew and probably wanted to turn and see how this sermon was affecting his family. Robert stole a glance at his mother. Her eyes looked dreamy. His dad was digging dirt out of his thumbnail. It was as if they hadn't woken up yet today. Sleepwalking, that was what they were doing.

The church creaked and the weight of the hot air seemed to double. The reverend's words were soon lost on Robert, as if the heat had dried up the meaning, leaving only husks of sound. He mentioned the sparrow again, but Robert's brain couldn't take the sense of the lesson in.

Reverend Gibbs paused to wipe his forehead. Robert wished the sermon were over, wished he were in the shade of a tree, away from the heat that choked the tiny church. "And let us pray especially for Matthew Steelgate's safe return." Everyone knelt and bowed their heads in prayer, knees knocking the prayer kneelers. "Dear God, please look out for Matthew—"

*"Screep!"* A sharp squeal cut the air. Robert jerked his head up. Reverend Gibbs glared at the congregation, his right hand held out as if pulled by a string, his left fist tight against his chest. His mouth opened and closed as if he were a fish on dry land. He looked as though he had been stabbed in the back.

*"Cheep! Cheep!"* he screamed. *"Rowf! Rowf! Nayyyy!"* His parish was agog with horror.

"He must be having a fit!" Robert's dad whispered.

Gibbs roared like a lion, pounded his right fist, then his left, against his chest. He gaped at the crowd, red-faced. A few children and even some adults couldn't stifle their nervous laughter. The reverend gasped twice, sucked in a hearty breath. His eyes focused and he wiped spittle from his lips and breathed in again.

"Lift up your hearts to the Lord," he said, sounding exhausted.

"We lift up our hearts," voices answered automatically.

Reverend Gibbs gestured. The choir sang the final hymn and followed him out of the church.

"It was too hot," Robert's dad said. "Must have woken up his epilepsy again."

Robert knew epilepsy was bad and the reverend had experienced other fits, but that had never before happened in church. The kids at school had joked that Robert would catch epilepsy from reading at recess. Epilepsy was a terrible affliction—a demon inside that made you shake and swear and sweat and gnash your teeth and froth at the lips like a dying calf. Doctors had to jam a piece of wood in your mouth to stop you from biting off your tongue.

The crowd filed out solemnly.

Reverend Gibbs waited at the door for his parishioners. He shook everyone's hands, even the children's. Robert was surprised at how clammy and wrinkled that hand was—as old and gray as a mummy's. He imagined he was shaking God's hand, and it was cold.

His family found a patch of shade under a nearly leafless birch tree, watching as the townspeople gathered in the churchyard. No one left for home; it was as though they expected a picnic.

The new man was the last to come out of the church. Gibbs winced when they shook hands. A blue, crackling bolt of energy shot from the stranger's palm. Robert blinked. Perhaps it was the sun's reflection off a cuff link. The man smiled, said a few words, then left. Gibbs stood with his hand still out, rubbing his fingers, his face pallid.

The stranger mixed with the crowd, nodding in a friendly manner. People seemed to know him. Robert watched his smooth, perfect movements. This man was sure of his step.

He spoke to Mr. Ruggles, who was standing with the war widows. The shopkeeper threw back his head and guffawed, the fat beneath his chin bouncing. The widows smiled eagerly, though with tight lips. Perhaps they didn't get the joke. The man tipped his hat, moved to another group.

"Who is that gentleman?" Robert's mother asked. "He looks familiar."

"He's new to town," his dad answered. "He lives on Skegi's old farm out north. Not sure what he'll do with that land; it's all sand and alkali sloughs. People have been talking about him. I'm not sure what his name is."

Then the man looked directly at Robert. A smile came to his lips. He waved like an old friend.

"I don't believe we've met," he said as he approached Robert's dad. He held out his hand. "My name is Abram Harsich."

They shook. The man tipped his hat to Robert's mom and leaned to look Robert in the eye. "And who might you be?" he asked, his voice gravelly. The skin of his face was pale white. His dark-lensed glasses had slipped down his nose, revealing red irises.

Robert gawked. He'd read in one of Uncle Alden's adventure magazines about albinos with skin as white as elephant tusks and eyes as red as a burning sun. Could this man be one?

"Don't you have a name, son?" Abram asked. His eyelashes were a ghostly silver.

"Uh . . . I'm Robert."

Abram's gaze penetrated like a searchlight into him. He seemed to be measuring Robert with his crimson eyes. "A good name," Abram announced, offering a gloved hand. Robert shook it. The man's fingers felt wiry and hard under the leather. Robert glanced at his hand, trying to figure out why Abram would wear gloves on such a hot day.

Abram rose to the height of Robert's parents. "I hope you'll come to the show this afternoon."

"Show?" Robert's dad asked.

"Oh, sorry," Abram said, "I assumed everyone knew. Word spreads so quickly in these small towns. I'm putting on a show in the Royal Theatre."

"A talkie?" Robert's mom asked. Robert heard the mistrust in her voice.

"No, Mrs. Steelgate. Not a talkie. A show of wondrous proportions." His smile widened. "Even Reverend Gibbs agreed to attend, so I guarantee it's not sinful. Merely a simple revelation of life's beauties. Dare I say, it might even be educational."

She seemed to relax. Maybe they would go, Robert thought. Into the theater, where the projector flashed pictures on the wall.

"What are you going to show us?" Robert's dad asked.

"A kaleidoscopic visual delight that I brought from the ancient tombs of Egypt." Abram bowed slightly. "Excuse me, I must prepare. It begins at two. There will be lemonade, tarts, and cookies for all. Mrs. Juskin and Mrs. Torence made the treats, kind hearts that they are."

He took a couple of steps and then turned back suddenly. His face was solemn. "I am sorry to hear about the disappearance of your son. I sincerely hope he is found soon. My prayers are with him. And with you."

Then he disappeared into the crowd.

# CHAPTER EIGHT

THE ROYAL THEATRE WAS A MAJESTIC HALL THAT HAD BEEN BUILT fifteen years before but had already aged by a century. Robert hadn't been inside since the doors had been hammered shut two years earlier. He was surprised at how fixed up the parlor was now. Abram had rehung the grand pine doors, swept off the steps, and reattached the head to the stone lion out front. It had been decapitated ages ago by a drunk driver from Eastend who'd lost control of his Model T.

Robert's anticipation grew. Abram had said something about the tombs in Egypt. Would there be camels in the desert? Men with sabers flashing in the sun? Maybe there'd be mummies and pharaohs.

Robert and his parents joined the line of people shuffling toward the theater. It was taking forever to get in. They were going to miss the beginning. Why was everyone walking so slowly?

Once inside, he was relieved to see that the show hadn't started yet. And it was as cool as a cave in the desert. He expected to hear water dripping from the walls and see stalactites and stalagmites jutting out like old, sharpened teeth. It was as though this were the first time in his life he'd ever been cool—a new, delicious sensation.

People filed between two Roman-style columns in the foyer, stopping to pick up treats from the war widows, who handed out their baking as though it were gold. He received a glass of lemonade, an oatmeal raisin cookie, and a pat on the head.

"It's nice of Mr. Harsich to do this," Robert's mom said. "And it's all free."

He was surprised at his mother's words. Not in a hundred million years had he expected her to set foot in the theater, and yet here she stood, sipping lemonade. He decided it was best not to point that out to her, lest she change her mind.

"It's a good gesture." Robert's dad chomped down the last of his cookie and wiped the crumbs from his bottom lip. "People need a break, if only for an afternoon."

They followed the crowd into the theater, passing two mummy tombs on the way. A skeleton hand reached out of one, frozen in mid-grab. Robert had seen them before when he'd sneaked into the Royal Theatre with his uncle Alden. They weren't real, but he longed to peek inside. Paintings of pharaohs with scarab amulets decorated the walls. "Old Man Spooky"—his real last name was Spokes—had built this place, then lost it to the bank after something called the big stock market crash. He'd also lost his wife to consumption. Now all Spooky did was drink, and sleep on the bench outside the hotel.

Standing in the aisle, Robert couldn't see past his dad. He had a great view of people's backs, arms, and legs. He worried that he might be missing some action on the screen. The room was packed. Kids laughed and ate as many cookies as they could get their hands on. Most everyone was still in their church clothes, lending an air of a special outing. This was wonderful fun, a party. They were make-believing that the sun wasn't outside, that a drought wasn't waiting for them. This was a new world, a safe place.

Robert's father cut a path to three velvet parlor seats. Robert took the one closest to the wall and thought, Sit down, everyone. You're all blocking my view! He wished he had a voice as loud as a trumpet and the gumption to use it.

They all continued chatting and laughing. A chandelier dangled high above, like an electrified web, pale lights flickering in the cool air. Robert glimpsed a flash of silver and gold at the front. He squirmed in his seat, trying different angles, but couldn't see anything else.

He sat back, shivering, partly from the excitement. He cocked his head, and this time he saw the projection screen. His eyes widened. It looked like a giant mirror. The townspeople's reflections were long or fat, as in a carnival fun house. Snakes in gold twisted and writhed along its edges. And dead center, at the top, was a large gold scarab, its eyes two emeralds. Robert had read that pharaohs wore such amulets as a symbol of immortality. So this mirror had to be from Egypt.

Colors shimmered in the mirror like rippling water. It's amazing! he thought. Absolutely amazing! It looked as though he could walk right through the mirror into a rainbow world. When he gazed directly at the surface, it appeared close enough to touch, but when he looked to the side, the mirror was where it was supposed to be—half a room away.

Several red clay jars were stacked below it. They seemed to have writing on their sides. They reminded him of the broken jar he'd touched in the sandhills. He squinted at them; then a flash drew his attention. Two glass batteries, half the size of apple crates, were wired to the mirror. Tiny bolts of captured lightning sparked inside. There was just too much to look at.

The lights dimmed, then brightened. Abram appeared at the center of the stage, seemingly out of nowhere. A young woman shrieked, then covered her mouth and giggled. "Oh, sorry, I'm so sorry," she said. Men around her laughed, and Abram grinned. Rubbing his gloved hands together, he waited until everyone took their seats. Soon there was only the squeaking of springs and scraping of feet.

Abram gestured dramatically toward the large mirror. "The Mirror of All Things. This bit of metal and glass is as ancient as our civilization, as old as the Ark of the Covenant. Maybe older. It will show you whatever you want to see."

"What's this about?" Robert asked. "I thought it was going to be an Egyptian show." Neither of his parents took their eyes off the mirror to answer.

Abram pointed, and the emeralds on the golden scarab glowed brightly. "Oh, Mirror of All Things, show us what we dream."

The lights dimmed all the way this time, and the room grew dark as night. A long, low noise reverberated through the walls. A familiar sound. After a few moments of slow struggle, Robert recognized it as the whistle of a distant train. It was the eerie cadence of time going by, of journeying to another country, of things passing on. It made him feel tired, as though he was about to slip into a dream.

Then the mirror flashed. The people of Horshoe caught their breath.

"I see rain," a man a few seats away exclaimed. "Glorious rain."

"And flowers," a woman said breathlessly.

"Dolls!" a girl peeped. "A closet full of dolls!"

Robert didn't see anything. The others gaped at the mirror, faces slack-jawed or agog with wonder. They *were* seeing something, but there was nothing for him. Just a dull gray. The mirror wasn't even reflecting light.

"Matthew," he heard his mother saying quietly. "Oh, Matthew. My dear Matthew."

Robert swallowed, an acidic taste in his mouth. His mom's faint voice was terrible and sad. Hearing his brother's name, Robert felt his guts flutter.

Abram stood, hands behind his back, watching the crowd. He looked happy, apparently content that everything was working properly. Robert still saw nothing—no flowers, no rain, no Matthew. The mirror must be broken, he thought.

Just then the gray behind the glass began rolling like storm-laden clouds. Winged shapes circled inside shadows. He couldn't look away; the mirror was the only thing that existed.

A figure appeared and moved close to the mirror's edge, walking with a lopsided limp. Robert dug his fingers into his legs as the form got closer. Go away! he thought. Go away! He heard grunting and a low rumbling, like ice cracking on a lake. He could make out the shape of a man, near enough that Robert heard his dragging footsteps. Finally he emerged from the fog. He was wearing an army uniform.

Robert's heart thumped hard in his chest. It was his uncle Edmund, who had died so long ago, whose picture Robert had committed to memory.

This was Edmund during the war, alive and breathing but badly injured. He had been hit by shrapnel; his uniform was tattered and bloody. He reached out, fumbled momentarily, and found the frame of the mirror, and it creaked as he leaned on it. Behind Edmund was the battlefield: Explosions blossomed brightly, sparks of gunfire dotted the land, smoke blended into storm clouds, wounded men screamed in pain.

Edmund looked back at the battlefield, then out again through the mirror. His face showed the confusion of a man who had staggered into unfamiliar territory. He squinted, scanned the crowd. He can see us! Robert thought.

Edmund found Robert, caught his eye for a moment, then swallowed hard, leaning forward so it seemed he might come right through the mirror. He waved weakly, his hand rising slightly above his hip. His mouth moved but produced no sound. Robert thought he was trying to tell him something.

I'm listening, Robert thought, I'm listening.

A shell shattered the ridge behind Edmund, sending a blast of heat over Robert. Edmund struggled to stay upright, gesturing desperately with one hand. His voice was muffled when he yelled, and it sounded as though he were saying "Ay-vil! Ay-vil!" He pointed at Abram, who had been standing a few feet from the mirror. "Ayvil! Ayvil!" Then Robert heard him more clearly: "Evil!"

Abram must have heard too, because his smile faded. He charged at the mirror.

*No!* Robert wanted to yell, but he couldn't force the word out of his mouth. Abram plunged his hand through the filmy barrier of the mirror and pierced Edmund's chest. It exploded with crimson light. Edmund screamed, his head thrown back, his hands thrust out in front, one flailing right through the mirror. Then he disappeared.

The mirror went black, and the audience woke with a shudder, as if startled by a loud noise. They glared at the stage like children whose toys had been taken away from them.

"The Mirror of All Things has finished its display," Abram announced, bowing. The lights brightened. Abram ran his hands across the glass and glanced at Robert, then back at the mirror.

In that moment Robert felt wrath, shot toward him like a bolt.

# CHAPTER NINE

T HE MIRROR NOW REFLECTED 259 BEWILDERED FACES, PEOPLE WHO looked as though they had just woken up in a strange place. Abram adjusted a lever behind the mirror, then laid it flat. Robert couldn't see the surface anymore, but it caught the chandelier's lights and cast them onto the ceiling, studding it with stars.

Abram turned to the townspeople. His smile was gone, and he seemed more like a man about to deliver a eulogy than perform a magic trick.

"I'm not finished yet. I have another surprise about something dear to your hearts. The very future of this community." He put his hands together as if he were about to pray. "Forgive me for becoming serious during this entertainment, but my topic is very important. I have but one message: Together we can end this drought."

The words were like stones cast into a pool; astonishment rippled through the crowd and over Robert.

"What does he mean?" his father asked.

"Allow me to explain," Abram said. "Many of you know me from church, and others have met me at my farm, but no one knows that I am, first and foremost, a meteorologist." He gestured toward the ceiling. "Meteorology, for those unfamiliar with the term, is the study of the atmosphere, of weather patterns, so that we can accurately predict the weather. It is a science in its infancy. I am a scholar who has learned how to influence the weather. What makes snow, hail, wind?" He paused.

Robert heard the wind whistling outside. He recognized that Abram was like the reverend, building words into a sermon.

"Long have I sought to understand these things. I have developed hypotheses that I have kept from my colleagues. Secrets. Horshoe is the perfect place to test my theories. With your help, we can make it rain as often and as hard as you wish. It is, of course, too late for this year's crop, but next year at this time we will be sitting with bins so full of wheat, and fields so stacked with hay, that the whole world will gaze in amazement."

He looked from face to face; his eyes pierced Robert, then passed by. In that moment Robert felt Abram's intensity, his belief in his own words. Potential, that was what Robert saw in those eyes. Promise.

"I know. I know. Fool's gold, you're thinking! You'd be daft not to." Abram's eyes narrowed. "But you are also thinking: What if he *can* make it rain? What if next year we could grow the crops we deserve?

"I will bring rain!" He pounded his fist into his palm, startling Robert. "I guarantee it. But only with your help. You've already witnessed the impossible reflected in a mirror. Soon the impossible will be real. Your fields will be green. I will show you how."

As the lights dimmed, Abram reached into one of the clay jars that had been sitting on the stage and cast a handful of red dust over the mirror. From a second jar Abram withdrew a palmful of blue dust. He tossed it into the floating red cloud. A cinnamon smell filled Robert's nostrils. He breathed it in, salivating. The dust thickened into a foglike smoke that split into three different trails. They glowed green, yellow, and violet, then changed colors and curled into a cylinder, which rotated, reminding Robert of a dazzling kaleidoscope. Again, the lonely wail of a distant train. He blinked and began to feel tired.

The cylinder was now brownish red. It grew to about twelve feet in height, a tower of earth-red bricks. Robert couldn't figure out where it had come from. It looked solid enough. How could Abram have made it appear from a handful of dust?

"This is Raithgan, the rainmill," Abram said. Four white vanes appeared near the top of the tower and spun counterclockwise. Abram pointed, and the spinning stopped. "Here"—he gestured at three spokes sticking out of the vanes—"are the containment filters that will hold a special liquid I call *vive,* short for vivification. *Vive* causes an atmospheric reaction that leads to the formation of heavy cumulous clouds, followed by rain, to put it simply."

It didn't sound all that simple to Robert. It was something only scientists would understand.

Tiny rain clouds formed over the tower, striking it with lightning bolts. Robert's arm hair stood straight up. It was *real* miniature lightning. It had to be. Not like the kind he'd seen in *Frankenstein,* a talkie Uncle Alden had taken him to.

"The process seeds the clouds, making them water-bearing.

The rainmill will continue to manufacture rain clouds until the motors are shut off. It will be a perpetual rain-making machine." He gestured again and the image froze. He turned back to the people.

"Impossible, right? I've shown you pretty pictures, tossed out some big words. You need something concrete. Something that isn't mist in the air." He passed his hand through the image of the rainmill. "You will have it.

"I have had numerous meetings with Mr. Samuelson, the manager of Horshoe Savings and Loan." Abram nodded at the banker and his wife, sitting in the front row. Cigar smoke plumed out of Samuelson's mouth. "I have shown him blueprints and projected crop yields. As you know, bankers are hardheaded when it comes to money, but we have hammered out an agreement. I'd like to ask him to come up and announce the terms of that deal."

Samuelson rose and lumbered toward the stage, his cigar flaring red. People in the front row pulled back their feet to avoid injury. *Pompous,* Robert thought. That word summed up everything about Samuelson. *Pompous, swaggering pooh-bah.*

The banker climbed the stairs at the middle of the stage, strode over to Abram, and turned to the audience. He wore a dress coat with tails; a large red sash held back his protruding stomach. Samuelson removed the cigar, tapped the ashes.

"I have examined Mr. Harsich's proposal with great care." His voice was deep and rough, vocal cords scarred by smoke. "I believe the rainmill is authentic. Its construction will create untold economic growth in our community. As long as a work crew is formed to aid Mr. Harsich, I will personally put every interest and loan payment due from those workers on hold until this date next year."

"My God," Robert's dad mumbled. "He can't be serious."

Heads turned, people muttered questions. Robert saw that Abram's and Samuelson's faces were split by wide, childlike smiles; the banker winked at Abram. The crowd's disbelieving noises grew to a senseless cacophony, so loud that Robert was tempted to cover his ears.

A man raised his arm and waved it. The din receded into a hissing of whispers and then silence.

"Yes," Abram said gently. "You have a question?"

"How do we know this thing will actually work?" the man asked.

The crowd drew a collective breath in shock. Robert squirmed off his seat and stood leaning against the wall. The speaker was Uncle Alden. His voice sounded distant and slightly garbled.

"I've read about other rainmakers who used airplanes and such to seed clouds. Far as I know, they never had any success."

"What's your name, sir?" Abram asked.

"Alden Bailey."

"Well, Mr. Bailey, you asked a good question. Thank you for that. I'm glad you asked it. But it's a question that will be answered only in time. I'm afraid everyone will need a little patience, too.

When Monday's edition of *The Horshoe Times* comes to your door, there will be a special article outlining our plans and the conditions of Mr. Samuelson's deal. I believe all this business can be dealt with satisfactorily on Monday. In the meantime, enjoy your lemonade and treats."

He clapped his hands, the image of the rainmill collapsed into the mirror, and the lights flickered on. All that remained on the stage were two men and a mirror.

"We should talk to him," Robert's father said. "Find out more about this deal."

Robert's mother nervously wrung her dress, stared at the mirror, and whispered, "I saw Matthew."

# CHAPTER TEN

**A** MASS OF MURMURING BODIES SHUFFLED INTO THE BRIGHT LIGHT OF A burning sun. They shaded their eyes, squinted at each other. Robert felt they were walking out of some imaginary place into the real world. Or perhaps it was the opposite, and they had just stumbled onto a strange planet devastated by a war with the sun. It burnt their skin, the fields, everything under its gaze. Maybe the real world, cool and inviting, was back inside the theater?

No one wanted to leave the front steps: They leaned against the railing, plugged up the passage. Some even turned around as if to go back inside. Robert was jostled by elbows and purses. The stink of underarm sweat wafted in the air. He wished he were taller; then maybe he wouldn't smell it.

Uncle Alden squeezed in beside Robert and his parents. "What a snake-oil trick," he hissed quietly, "all smoke and mirrors."

Robert's dad remained silent, pulling Robert by the hand, guiding him through the crowd. Then his grip loosened and Robert looked up. His parents were gone, swallowed by the mass of people.

Robert stepped over feet, around legs, and got too close to the war widows. One reached out to pull him to her bosom or do something equally frightening, so he ducked and launched himself into the forest of arms and legs. He figured he'd be able to spot his parents from the other side of the street.

Escape was only inches away. He watched his step, avoided several more elbows, and finally bumped into a heavyset man in a suit.

"It's all for nothing," he heard the man announce hoarsely, "all of it."

Robert knew the voice. He looked up to see Reverend Gibbs, hunched over, holding his side. People avoided him as though he were a big stone in the middle of a field.

"It's futile," he said.

"What?" Robert asked him. "What did you say?"

The reverend raised his head, revealing wild, red-rimmed eyes. Robert had once seen a stray dog crazy with rabies, and its eyes had looked like that. Gibbs blinked, and his pupils remained dilated.

"Who's there?" he said.

"It's Robert Steelgate, sir."

The reverend blinked again, recognition lighting up his face. "Robert. Hello. It's . . . it's good to see you."

"Why is it all for nothing?" Robert asked. "Did you see something in the mirror?"

The reverend's upper lip trembled. "You be a good boy," he whispered. "Stay close to your parents, now. Remember your brother. Keep close and God will watch you. He will."

Reverend Gibbs stumbled past Robert and limped down the boardwalk, his feet thumping on the wood.

"Sometimes faith breaks," a gentle voice said. "It's always a pity."

Robert started and whipped around to find Abram standing there, watching the reverend head up the hill toward the rectory.

"You've caught my interest," the man told him.

"What?" Robert looked for his parents. Everyone seemed frozen and silent, as if they had been turned to pillars of salt.

"You represent something. I don't know exactly what." Abram leaned closer. He smelled of lemons. "I do have a very important scientific question to ask you. It would help immensely if you answered truthfully. You do want to help, don't you?"

Robert was confused. What could Abram possibly want to hear? He nodded solemnly.

"Good." Abram's eyes became the only thing Robert could see. Flecks of gold swirled through the man's pupils. "Tell me what you saw in the mirror today."

Robert's limbs froze. Only his lips moved.

"Nothing," he said, "just darkness."

Abram narrowed his eyes; a line creased his forehead. "Nothing? But I know everyone sees something; it's only human. That mirror is the ultimate development in the science of mesmerism. To look at its reflection is to look at your own desires. Your needs. But some can see farther. Into other places. Are you sure you didn't see even a shadow, perhaps? A man on a battlefield? Hear a message from beyond?"

Robert closed his eyes. His heart was racing, his throat dry. It would be bad if Abram knew what had appeared in the mirror. It would make Robert feel like a traitor somehow. I can't tell him, Robert thought. I can't. I can't.

He swallowed. "Rain," he answered, spitting out the word as though he were dislodging a stone from his throat. "I saw rain in my father's fields. Falling really soft."

Abram stared for an eternity. Robert met his eyes, trying to look as honest as possible. Finally Abram nodded. His gloved hand rested on Robert's shoulder with the weight of a crow.

"You're a very curious young man, aren't you? And I say *man* because you're not really a boy anymore. You're getting too tall, growing too old."

Robert didn't think he was old or tall.

"I feel sorry for you. One morning you will get up and your dreams will stay in your pillow." His hand tightened. "What if I told you that some individuals are born without a soul and have to wander for thousands and thousands of years searching for a way to fill that void? They become pharaohs, forcing slaves to build pyramids, or rise from peasant to emperor and command vast conquering armies, or compel tribes in the jungle to worship them. And still they feel empty. What if I told you that? Would you believe me?"

Robert looked into Abram's pale face, his all-knowing eyes. It had to be true. Those eyes had seen battles and wars and stars dying in the heavens. Robert believed. He felt it in the center of his heart, but he sensed he should never admit it. Better to hide that knowledge, the same way he had hidden his John Carter books.

"No," Robert said, trying to sound confident. "What you're saying isn't true. People don't live that long."

Abram smiled and released his grip. "You're right," he said, "you're right."

The crowd came to life, moving and talking again. A farmer looked startled to see Abram standing right in front of him. Abram smiled, extended his arm, and shook hands, calling the man by name.

Robert watched Abram work his way through the people, shaking more hands, patting shoulders, jesting. He even kissed one lady's proffered fingers.

# CHAPTER ELEVEN

THE SUN HAD BAKED THE WHEAT GOLDEN BROWN, TURNING THE STALKS hollow and hard. The heads swayed in the wind, moving in waves. Even though Robert lived thousands of miles from the nearest ocean, he was sure the field looked like one. The patches of brown dirt could be islands.

The harvest would be soon; his dad had told him as much. In fact, his father had been telling him a lot these days, talking non-stop as they worked on the tractor.

"So I dove into the swimming hole," he babbled, "dog-paddled around, and jumped out crawling with leeches—clinging to my underarms, my chest, even my privates. My mother grabbed the cigarette out of the hired man's mouth and burnt them little monsters off, one by one. Yee-ouch!"

Robert shivered. He'd once had a creek leech on his elbow and it had inspired a week of nightmares. "Did you have any blood left?"

"I was pale as milk. Speaking of blood, that reminds me . . ." And he launched into another tale, about a hockey game where the puck had banked off the rink boards, hit a wooden post, and smacked into a politician's forehead. Robert's father laughed his guts out about that one.

Still chuckling, he undid a cap on the engine and peered in. "Oh, for crying out loud!" he exclaimed. "The tractor needs more oil. We're gonna have to head to town. I was planning on going later anyway; might as well go now. You want to come along?"

"Sure. I'll tell Mom."

His dad waved away the suggestion. "Let's surprise her. Bring back a licorice stick. She loves those."

Within a few minutes they were in the roadster. Robert watched out the window as the land rolled by. He'd worked really hard over the past week, fetching tools, helping with the chores, and mending fences. They'd spent hours repairing the grain wagon, tightening every screw and plugging every hole so the wheat wouldn't drain out.

His parents had been in an extraordinarily good mood the whole time. They'd kept talking about the fun they'd had at the theater. Robert felt sick when he remembered his experience. He wasn't sure if he'd ever go inside that building again. When he thought about Uncle Edmund appearing in the mirror and pointing at Abram, he got a brassy blood taste in his mouth, as though he had cut his finger and sucked on it.

He looked at the horizon. It was so far away. Everything was small in the distance. Easy to lose things here, he thought.

"Will they ever find Matthew?" Robert asked.

His dad didn't answer. He just squinted down the road, grinning as if he were seeing that puck hit the politician again.

"Do you think they'll find Matthew?" Robert persisted, struggling to make his voice louder.

His father pinched his lips together, as though he'd tasted something sour. "What? Matthew?" He paused. "Yes. They will. Saw that sergeant in town the other day. He said they're still working on it. I told him to do the best he could. It'll be fine, Robert. Don't you worry. Just think about what's behind the candy counter in town. I'll get your mom a licorice stick, but what do you want? No, don't tell. Surprise me."

Robert wanted to ask more about Matthew, but his mouth was watering. A black jawbreaker would be good right now. Or a lemony-tasting sugar candy. He shook his head. There was something wrong with his mind, the way he kept daydreaming about things he wanted: candy and firecrackers and vanilla milkwhips. Every moment was filled with daydreams. Too many of them.

His dad turned sharply down Horshoe's access road, tires skidding. He let out a laugh. "This darling sure steers well."

Robert was silent as they crossed the tracks. On the west side of town he saw the school. In a few weeks he'd be back inside that single room, writing in his scribbler or memorizing multiplication tables. School started on a Monday. He wished he could remember what day it was right now. He'd looked at the Cypress Oil Company calendar that morning. It had been a day of rest, he remembered.

"Shouldn't we be going to church?"

"Your mom has baking to do, son," his dad said quickly.

"She's making apple pies. Just think of that. I can't remember the last time we had apple pie with cinnamon. And a big piece of cheddar cheese on the side."

Robert pictured the apple pie, steam rising from the hole in the center of the pastry, the sugary apples cooked to perfection inside. He wiped his mouth. He had to stop dwelling on these things.

He thought about his mom. She would be at home now, in the kitchen, baking the pies. Or washing dishes and setting the plates upside down in the cupboard so they wouldn't catch the dust. Upside-down dishes. The image stuck in his head. Everything was becoming upside down. His parents should be sad now, wishing for Matthew to come home. Instead, they talked only nonsense and laughed too loudly.

There were several cars and trucks on Main Street, and a few wagons. People streamed in and out of the hotel, the pool parlor, and the grocery store. Robert wondered if it hadn't been a field day or a parade day and they'd missed it. His dad steered around three men jabbering away in the middle of the road and parked in front of the bank. A line of people stood there, waiting in front of a table on the boardwalk.

Robert's dad snapped his fingers. "Oh, yes, *that's* why I wanted to come to town today. I need to sign up for that deal. Come on, son."

He jumped out of the roadster. Robert followed him, and they joined a row of about fifteen men. There were unshaven cowboys from the Speirs Ranch in the Cypress Hills, hired hands from the Big Farm, sandhill sheep herders, even some hobos with blanket rolls slung over their shoulders. The lineup ended at a table where the war widows were handing out lemonade and cookies. Standing beside them, shaking each person's hand, was Mr. Samuelson.

The closer Robert got to the front of the line, the more uneasy he became. He didn't like the raucous, tumbling laughter that rolled out of Samuelson every time he shook a hand. There was no sign of Abram.

When they reached the very front, Robert knew what was worrying him the most. He wanted to grab his father's arm and pull him away, because signing your name was like putting a piece of yourself down on paper. It was a promise. For all eternity.

His father, grinning, reached for the pen and dipped it in ink.

Don't, Dad, Robert thought. He even lifted his arm to stop him, but it was too late. His father had scratched out his signature and immediately shook Samuelson's hand, as though they'd been buddies all their lives.

"You're a good man, Steelgate," Samuelson said. "Great to have you aboard."

Robert had heard his father curse Samuelson a thousand times. Now they were shaking hands. Samuelson muttered a joke so Robert couldn't hear it. Robert's dad burst into laughter; then he steered Robert over to the lemonade and cookies.

"Hi, Robbie," Mrs. Juskin said. "Looking forward to having you back in class. You're a good student."

Robert silently clutched the cookie in his right hand and nodded to her, because it was better not to say anything. His father had already finished his lemonade and cookie and was wiping his mouth. He led Robert back to the roadster, saying, "Let's go get that candy."

"I don't want any." Robert couldn't believe what he'd just heard himself say.

His father laughed. "All the more for me and Mom," he said, striding jauntily to the pool parlor.

Robert poured the lemonade onto the dusty road and dropped the cookie behind one of the roadster's back wheels. He watched as the line in front of the bank grew even longer.

# CHAPTER TWELVE

Sky was the first God. Robert knew there was only one God and he had a Son who was also God, but there were gods who had vanished: the gods of thunder, of fire, of the wide oceans, of the earth. The ones God was talking about when He commanded, "You shall have no gods before me. No false idols."

Robert stood in a sparse wheat field of Uncle Alden's. The sky was cradled by the Cypress Hills on one side, and ahead lay the flat prairie. Storm clouds had gathered like an army in the distance, bolts of lightning displaying their strength. He had never seen clouds like this, as black as the hide on an Angus bull. The air was hot and humid, waiting to be split asunder.

"I'll be damned if there isn't hail in them clouds," Uncle Alden said. He stood a few feet away from Robert, sweat on his brow. He had been working on the plow, trying to sharpen shovels worn from being dragged endlessly through the soil and banged into rocks. He looked down at his nephew. "Sorry for the swearing, pal. I've got the addled brains of a peacock some days."

Robert shrugged. He had to admit to himself that he enjoyed hearing the swear words—they were real, weighty. Old and powerful. They grabbed your attention. Of course, there was Someone's attention you wouldn't want to attract. "God might zap you with lightning," Robert warned.

Uncle Alden laughed. "I'll lie low next time," he promised. "Or carry a lightning rod. Maybe sell the electricity. Could be a new line of work." He grinned, then shook his head. "Guess I shouldn't laugh too hard on a day like this. That storm's gonna make ol' Reverend Gibbs's funeral a real mess. Looks like it's heading for Horshoe."

Robert was at his uncle's farm because his parents were attending the funeral. His mother had given him a choice: come to the service or go to Uncle Alden's. It was an easy decision. He didn't want to see a dead person in a casket or hear the weeping and gnashing of teeth he'd read about in the Bible.

And what if it all started him to weeping and gnashing about Matthew? He might never stop. He felt sad every morning when he got up and saw that Matthew's bed was empty, the sheets straight and neat. Once he'd awakened and thought they were mussed up, but that was a long time ago and had to have been part of a dream.

His mom didn't mind Robert coming out here so much now. She had forgiven and forgotten all her brother's sins. She was not as . . . what was the word? *Judgmental*. She didn't sit in judgment as often as before.

"We'd better lock the chickens up," Uncle Alden said. He was thin as a straight line, striding toward the barn. Robert followed.

They chased chickens into the coop, running half stooped, stretching their arms out near the ground as though they were pretending to be airplanes.

"One year I was too slow," his uncle said, hooking the latch on the coop door, "didn't get them all, and the brainless birds couldn't find cover. They were flattened dead as doornails by hail. Every bone in their bodies broken. Couldn't even make soup out of them. So I rolled them up and sold them as doormats." He paused. "Ha! Just kidding you, Robert."

Robert laughed out loud. He bent over, held his breath, and nearly broke into a fit of giggles. It had been a long time since he'd laughed like that.

Next Robert and Uncle Alden walked out to the pasture. Uncle Alden's herd was small: ten cows, four calves, three steers, and one old Hereford bull named Mino. "I'll head the rotters this way and you steer 'em to the gate." His uncle clapped his hands. "Steer 'em! Get that? It's a pun. Those are steers and you're going to ..."

Robert gave him a blank look.

"Oh, never mind," his uncle huffed. He jogged to the far end of the pasture, his cowboy boots barely touching the ground. Robert grinned at the sight of his uncle's gawky running. Careful, he wanted to yell, your legs might come flying off.

Steer the steers ... "Wait," he said, "I get it." But Uncle Alden was out of earshot.

Robert examined the hills above him. His uncle had said the Ice Age formed those hills; there were indented rings where the ice had retreated, season by season. He imagined ice grinding everything flat across the land, pushing people ahead of it, south to the States.

The world was like a big clock, every day a second of time, every year a minute. His life was a blink in the passing of all that time. Perhaps one day the ice would return. He pictured it. Nothing but ice. Horshoe covered in ice. The roads, the fields all ice, packing everything flat. Like a huge, cold hand pressing down on the earth.

"Hey, Don Quixote," Uncle Alden yelled, "it would be helpful if you got behind the cows instead of standing around in the middle of the pasture."

Robert shook his head, mumbled, "Sorry," then circled into position. Why was his uncle calling him Don Coyote?

The pasture narrowed into an alleyway that led to the barn, a long, rectangular building with an aging roof. He wondered if the hail would strafe it like the bullets of a warplane.

When they guided the animals into the barn, the old bull was at the end of the line. He shook his shoulders and belly as though he were trying to drive off an army of flies. He slammed his horns against the gate and attempted to turn around, but the alley wasn't wide enough. Uncle Alden grabbed the bull's tail and twisted. "Hyaa!" The bull then smacked the fence with his massive shoulder and two posts broke, giving him room to turn. He faced them, snorting.

He'd always been a friendly bull, shuffling around the pasture.

Robert had even petted him. But now the bull's eyes were wild, as though the Devil were riding him. The bull dug in his feet, bawled once, and charged ahead, knocking Uncle Alden to the ground.

He lay still. Robert ran to his side, worried that he'd been badly hurt.

His uncle smiled. "Please excuse me whilst I swear," he said. "Damn. Damn! Damn bull!" he ranted as he struggled to his feet, wiping off his shirt. "Close the barn door and let him stay out. He can shelter by the tree, if he thinks of it. His head is thick enough he should be safe, in any case. Speaking of shelter, we'd better get home."

They jogged out of the barnyard. Wind hissed between the shingles, making boards rattle, saying, *Hello, I'm here, guess what's following me.* Behind them the clouds had switched direction and were coming straight for the farm, curling in on themselves. Robert found it odd how black they were. He ducked into the house behind his uncle, who forced the door closed. Robert was relieved to be inside Uncle Alden's home.

They sat at the table. Books lined the shelves by the windowsill, were piled next to the large mahogany radio. Others were stacked on the floor. Magazines with names like *Weird Tales* and *Suspense Detective* had been scattered in a corner near Uncle Alden's easy chair. Robert knew Uncle Alden had even written stories for a few of the magazines.

His uncle clicked on the mahogany RCA Victor radio and

spun the dial. All he got was grumbling and roaring, as though the box were broadcasting the voice of the storm, getting closer and louder.

"Well, wouldn't that frost your petunias," he said, switching it off. "We're missing *The Shadow*."

It had been a long time since Robert had sat near his uncle's radio, eyes closed, turning the words into pictures in his mind. His mother didn't let him listen at home. Their radio, like everything else on the farm, had to have a "good" purpose: to hear the weather, the price of beef, or announcements from the government.

"Well, I feel sorry for that ol' reverend," Uncle Alden said, "a bad ticker and epilepsy. He was a stodgy sky pilot but not too overbearing, though most of what he said sounded like barking. Hard time they'll have getting some other sucker with a collar out here. Who'd leave the East for all this dust?"

Robert wasn't sure how to respond. This was adult talk, but then, his uncle had never differentiated between Robert and older people. He decided to shrug, the way his dad often did when neighbors chatted about the weather.

"You finish the John Carter book?" his uncle asked.

"I read it three times."

"Jeez, kid, you must be a whiz. I'll smuggle you a few more. Maybe Jules Verne. There's one where these guys get captured by a submarine captain and taken on a ocean journey: *Twenty Thousand Leagues Under the Sea*. Right up your alley."

The thought of a new book made Robert vibrate with excitement. "Submarines? Are there whales?"

"Whales? Of course, and giant squid with tentacles a hundred feet long. One grabs on to the submarine and tries to drag it to the ocean floor, so Captain Nemo gets a . . ." He stopped. Winked. "I better not give anything else away. I can see you'd like to read that one."

Robert frowned but understood; it wasn't good to know the ending. It stole some of the magic.

"Did I tell you about the book I'm reading now?" Uncle Alden asked. "About Thermopylae?"

Robert shook his head.

"You'd love it. It's a history of battles. Thermopylae was this mountain pass in Greece. In 480 B.C., Xerxes, the Persian king, invaded with two hundred thousand fighters, including the Immortals, his crack troops. Three hundred Spartan hoplites and their king, Leonidas, held them off at Thermopylae—they must have been tough. They battled for three days, long enough to allow the rest of the Greek army to escape. Then the Persians crept down a secret path and surrounded the Spartans. They fought to the last man."

Thermopylae. Robert ran the name through his head. It made him feel as though he were traveling back in time. He heard the clash of spears. Saw the hoplites raise their shields. Then he thought of the trenches in the Great War.

"Was Thermopylae like the battle for Vimy Ridge?" he asked.

Uncle Alden nodded. "Yeah, I guess. I never thought of it that way. Except we won—well, took the ridge from the Huns, that is. No one else had been able to, not the French or the British. Only the Canadians did it. We became a country then—I don't care what the history books say; that's when we proved our mettle to the world. We paid a heavy price."

Sadness made Uncle Alden look about ten years older. Robert knew he was thinking about his brother, Edmund. Robert wanted to ask more questions about Edmund but decided not to interrupt his uncle's thoughts.

A blast of wind hit the side of the house, so Uncle Alden went to the window. "It's almost here! It's a bruiser, too, like the hand of the Devil. Maybe there *is* an Armageddon."

Robert had read about that in the Bible. That was when everyone started fighting and the Devil was unchained and let loose upon the world and the Four Horsemen of the Apocalypse went out chopping off heads and releasing diseases. He knew it was a bad, bad time that was coming in the future. He had read about it several times because it was exciting—a great ending to all the stuff that happened in the Good Book.

He stared out the window. Armageddon clouds, with lightning horsemen galloping along their underbelly.

"I saw clouds like that at the theater," his uncle said. Robert held really still, not wanting to miss a word. "In that mirror. First flowers and rain, all this beautiful malarkey, then I saw those clouds. Black as molasses."

Robert felt feverish. The air was too hot and close, as though the storm were pushing it through the cracks in the walls.

"What . . . what did you see?" Robert asked.

"Clouds. Thunder. And guns and . . . it looked like Vimy Ridge. . . . For a moment I heard my brother yelling a warning. Even thought I saw him. Quite the magic trick."

Robert whispered, "But I saw him too."

Uncle Alden went pale. "You what?"

"I saw Uncle Edmund. In his uniform. He was at the war. The great one. And he was yelling, 'Evil.'"

"You didn't even know Uncle Edmund."

"I look at his picture every day," Robert said. "I've even had dreams about him."

"What kind of dreams?"

Robert looked down at the table. "Just dreams about the war, about being a hero. Then I saw him in the mirror. What do you think he was warning me—us—about?"

Uncle Alden tapped his fingers on the table. He cleared his throat. "I saw Edmund's body. He was dead. And dead people don't come back. That's one lesson I learned in the war. You've been staring at Edmund's picture too much, that's all. You've got an imagination the size of Texas. It wasn't magic." Uncle Alden wagged his finger at Robert, as though he were chastising him. "Abram's a trickster; he'd sell you the steam from your own pee. I know he suckered people into signing up for his work teams."

"Dad signed up," Robert offered.

Uncle Alden shook his head sadly. "I . . . well, I don't know what to think of that. There was some kind of Mesmer stuff going on with that mirror. It was all backlighting and swirling colors so different people saw different things, depending on where they were sitting." He paused. "But I saw the clouds. Others saw flowers and green crops. I saw clouds." He faltered. "It was a trick, Robert, don't worry your head." Uncle Alden put a comforting hand on Robert's shoulder. "A parlor trick," he said with finality.

Something cracked into the roof, startling Robert, and a moment later came a *thunk thunk thunk* that grew into a constant, heavy drumming.

"Hail." Uncle Alden laughed breathlessly. "Just what I need."

# CHAPTER THIRTEEN

THE BULL'S EARS WERE BLEEDING, AND SO WAS HIS NOSE. HIS EYES were glassy, cold marbles. He had fallen onto his side. The light inside that kept him moving, snorting, and rummaging for food had been hammered out. A few melting hailstones, about half the size of Robert's fist, decorated the bull's body. The ground was moist.

"Mino," Uncle Alden said quietly. "He's gone. I should have chased him in. I've never heard of a hailstorm killing a bull. They've got such thick skulls." Mino had been smart enough to stand by the tree but had found little protection.

"He's very dead," Robert said. The bull's hide was wet, and drops of blood had formed here and there, like red tears. His ribs showed, as though the hail had pounded away his flesh.

"I'll pull him to the dump yard with the tractor," Uncle Alden said. "He was a good bull. A good guy. I shoulda chased him in." He sighed loudly. "We better see if there's anything left of the wheat."

He tramped across the pasture toward his crop. Robert tried to keep up with the long-legged, desperate stride of his uncle. They stopped at the fence line.

One word entered Robert's head: *devastation*. The crop had been flattened, as if a giant had crushed it underfoot. Every stalk of wheat lay against the ground, broken to pieces. He knew this was a bad, bad thing to have happen.

Uncle Alden squeezed his hands into fists. "I'll be damned," he said, softly, so it didn't even sound like swearing. "I'll be good and damned."

# CHAPTER FOURTEEN

**H**ARVEST WAS IN FULL GEAR.

Robert was helping his father, piling the sheaves into stooks, while the threshing machine growled fifty yards away, a big metal monster that devoured wheat. It hissed and banged and breathed steam and spat the kernels into a pile.

This was Harvest, and that was a word that needed a capital H—it had meaning and weight. Meals, the start of school, even sleep—nothing was as important as Harvest. This was the first time he had stayed home from class. His parents had always said he was too small, but his body was now growing into a man's, and they wanted him there.

Which was nice.

Robert was sad about missing the first two weeks of school, because sometimes they studied other countries and history—and even Mrs. Juskin couldn't make that stuff boring. He was happy not to see her, though. She was a plump spider, sitting at her desk, waiting to bite any student who didn't pay attention.

For Harvest he had to get up early and work hard and long, until it felt as though his body would fall apart, as though everything inside had been sweated out and he was nothing but a shell. Then the sun would go down and they would go home to a deep sleep. Harvest was a demigod with special commands to be obeyed.

Maybe building the pyramids had been just like Harvest— work that *had* to be done. He pictured row after row of slaves, their brown backs sweating as they hauled giant blocks of stone up half-built pyramids. The Sphinx sitting like a lion waiting for the end of the world. Pharaoh Ramses watching from his chariot or litter, the Egyptian sun as hot as a forge, reflecting off the Nile.

"It's not the worst crop I've ever seen," Robert's dad said, clapping a hand on his son's shoulder. Robert had to run the words through his head a few times before he understood them. His dad watched Uncle Alden and the three hired men work away at the fallen wheat. They were threshers. *Threshers*. Robert liked the word. It sounded old, as though it came from the Bible. Let us be threshers of men. Or was that fishers?

"It's not as tall as sunflowers," Robert said matter-of-factly. The wheat was sparse and only reached his hips, unlike that in the fields he'd dreamed about from time to time, where he would traipse through the wheat, the stalks blocking the sun. But his dad was happy with it, and that was good. His dad had been really happy for a while now.

"We'll get back what we put into it and a bit more. Arnold at the elevator said the price might be going up a couple cents. Something to do with Russia."

Robert nodded. They were talking adult talk now and it

seemed more natural. He thought about Russia, a big, majestic country. The Cossacks lived there: fighters and cavalrymen. What was their connection to Horshoe grain?

"We don't have to pay our loan; that eases the burden. Didn't even have to use butter on the tractor's axles this year. Real grease all the way." His dad motioned toward Uncle Alden, who was feeding a stook into the threshing machine. "Your uncle seems better now. Terrible shame about his crop. Just plain ol' bad luck. He should go for that deal with Samuelson—he'd be in good shape then." Robert's dad rubbed his jaw thoughtfully. "Well, we should get back to the sheaves. No rest for the wicked."

The phrase sounded odd to Robert. It wasn't a saying his father had ever used before. Robert leaned down and grabbed a sheaf of wheat.

They worked as the dull red sun crept across the cloudless sky toward the horizon. When dusk turned the world gray, they set down their tools, stopped the growling of the threshing machine, and headed for the wagon. Uncle Alden held Robert with his stained, bleeding hands and lifted him into the box. His uncle's face was grim and tired, as though he'd gone sleepless for days. He sat silently beside Robert.

His father aimed the wagon straight toward the sun. It was like riding in a tunnel, a tunnel that led home, where his mother would have supper on the table: potatoes and carrots and peas, and maybe chicken. And she would have that strange, calm smile that made him feel more uncomfortable as each day passed.

"You read that book yet?" his uncle asked.

Robert shook his head. "Too busy. And it's dark when we get home."

"Sneak a candle upstairs. Your imagination is like a muscle; you have to keep it exercised."

"Okay," Robert said, but getting a candle would be tricky. And he really was tired at night. Exhausted. He had decided that people needed more sleep as they got older. Then, eventually, they slept forever.

"You hear about the dinosaurs in Alberta?"

Robert turned his head; his heart sped up. "Live ones?"

"Yeah, a *Tyrannosaurus rex* ate two politicians in Red Deer. Swallowed them whole." Uncle Alden chuckled gruffly. "I kinda made that up. But they did find a whole stack of fossils. Can't dig a fence hole there without hitting a dinosaur bone."

"Are there eggs?" Robert asked.

"Most probably. Reminds me of a story I wrote about a guy finding an egg and it hatches and he feeds this meat-eating dinosaur until it grows up and starts gobbling everyone in town."

"That sounds like a great story!"

"It'd be greater if I could sell it. Can't sell my wheat. Maybe I'll make my living as a writer!" He laughed.

The wagon bounced along, and Robert imagined the dinosaur egg cracking open, a green, scaly snout poking through the shell.

His uncle leaned in close. "Your parents ever talk about Matthew?"

"No." Just hearing someone else mention his brother's name gave Robert an immense feeling of relief. He peeked over his shoulder. A thresher was riding up front, chatting with his father. Robert moved even nearer to his uncle. "It's like he was never here."

"People are forgetting things. I asked know-it-all Ruggles if there was anything new in the investigation into Matthew's disappearance, and he said, 'Who?' It took a few minutes for him to remember. Others have forgotten, too. All they think about is this windmill. Oh, pardon me, *rain*mill. Guess the Mountie has poked his nose around, but nothing's ever come of it. Wish I could find some logical explanation."

Robert nodded. It was hard to think about Matthew. He needed to wait until Harvest was done. Then he'd be able to think again. To dream again. He was silent the rest of the trip.

The next morning he was up at dawn, home at dusk. On Sunday, he slept in. He hadn't intended to, but neither of his parents awakened him. When he went downstairs, his mother was pounding dough. She hit it like a punching bag, humming to herself. It took a few moments for her to notice Robert.

"So, you're up, Sunshine! What are you going to do with your day off?"

Robert shrugged. "I didn't know I was getting a day off."

"It's a day of rest." She draped a towel over the dough and set it near the window. "Unless you're making bread, of course. But that's not really work." Her hands were white with flour.

"Where's Dad?"

"He went to the rainmill. They started working on it a few weeks ago, and he wants to do his part. I gave him enough cheese and bread to last him the whole day."

Robert wasn't sure what to think about his dad stopping Harvest to work on the mill. Even Sunday wasn't usually a big enough day to stop Harvest.

Robert spent the day wandering around the farm, playing with the kittens in the hayloft, exploring the dry creekbed for signs of frogs. Later he crept upstairs and tried to read some of *Twenty Thousand Leagues Under the Sea*, but the words only made him tired.

At suppertime, his father walked in with an empty lunch basket. "The mill is taking shape," he announced. "Abram says everything's turning out fine. People are pitching in. It's quite the sight."

Robert's mother set a plate of steaming cabbage rolls on the table. "Who was there?"

"Ruggles, the Wicksons, Samuelson, Charlie Kreklau, the Vaganskis, the Wallace brothers—they brought their Clydesdales. Those horses are amazing! Hagan and his sons were there, that short guy who lives on the bench, even some hobos showed up; I shared some of my bread with them. . . . Most everyone was there. And Abram, of course."

"So who *wasn't* there?" The question was spoken softly, but Robert had the feeling it was really important to his mom.

"Old Man Spooky, the Hereford Hill hermit, all of the Chinamen, but they're foreigners, and . . . your brother wasn't there, either."

Robert looked at his mom and was surprised to see she was smiling. "I wish he'd grow up." She shook her head. "He was always juvenile. No wonder he's still a bachelor—he's got to just grow up and accept his responsibilities."

They ate, and all the while Robert thought about his uncle. He seemed grown up enough. He shaved, swore, smoked a pipe. Even chewed tobacco. Just because he read a lot of books didn't mean he wasn't grown up, Robert decided.

The next day, Robert was up with the sun and on the wagon, working hard. And so it went for the following two weeks, until all the wheat was in the bins or hauled to the elevators. Muscles had grown in his arms. He felt stronger and older, as though a birthday had passed while he had been helping.

And he hadn't had one dream in all that time.

# CHAPTER FIFTEEN

**R**OBERT CUT THROUGH THE OLD SLOUGH ON THE SCHOOL grounds, walking over what was now caked and cracked earth. Several clumps of dried bulrush pointed skyward, their sausage-shaped heads billowing with fluff. He searched for dinosaur tracks but found only rocks. He was in the wrong province, he told himself. Saskatchewan had nothing but rocks, Russian thistles, and sand. Uncle Alden had said there were loads of dinosaur bones in Alberta. Robert would give anything to toss on a wide-brimmed hat, walk straight to Alberta, and dig. Maybe he'd find the jaw of a *Tyrannosaurus rex*.

He aimed for the door of Horshoe's one-room school. Mrs. Juskin probably wouldn't ever talk about dinosaurs. She mostly taught numbers, reading, writing, and more numbers. The lessons in their readers never had anything to do with prehistoric times.

He was late, so he carefully opened the door and peeped through the crack. Twenty-four boys and girls sat at their desks, facing the front. Mrs. Juskin was writing on the chalkboard. She didn't take disruption lightly. Robert liked that word—*disruption*—there was something unstable about it, as though it were about to explode. He sneaked to his seat, relieved that she hadn't noticed his tardiness.

All the other seats were full, which surprised him. There wasn't a place left for Matthew. Perhaps they had moved his desk to the shed outside. Worse yet, Robert couldn't remember which row his brother had sat in.

Someone had scribbled "I will not pull ponytails" a hundred times on the smaller chalkboard. *Lines:* It was a word that inspired fear in Robert's heart. Mrs. Juskin was a firm believer that writing the same sentence over and over again would correct a student's bad behavior. To him, it was a crazy waste of time to follow a sentence with the same sentence. That would never tell a story.

The king of England glared down from a picture above the chalkboard, making sure the pupils paid attention to their lessons. Below him was Mrs. Juskin. She really could look like a spider waiting to strike. Her frozen marble eyes scanned for infractions. If you were loud, or a smart aleck, she quickly snapped the yardstick across your head. Robert had been smacked once when he'd asked whether God ever slept. Since God had rested on the seventh day of creation, Robert reasoned that He probably slept. It had been a logical question; a good one, even. Instead of an answer, *smack!* on the back of his skull. "Impertinent child."

The blow would have stung more if she hadn't said *impertinent*. The word echoed inside his head. Now, whenever he heard it, he thought of the smacking ruler. He used to use the word whenever he thought Matthew was getting out of line.

Matthew had never been smacked. He had always sat up straight. Mrs. Juskin had even entrusted him with telling her when her coffee was ready on the potbellied stove. And when her bacon was done at lunch. He had been a good pupil, and he'd made lots of friends, too. More than Robert ever had.

He wondered if his dream about Matthew being raised by coyotes could be real. It didn't seem that likely anymore—why would a coyote raise a human kid? Matthew was probably dead and would never come back. But they hadn't had a funeral; therefore, he might still be alive.

Mrs. Juskin banged her pointer on the desk. Everyone looked up, expecting a reprimand. Instead, she seemed peaceful, as though her stomach were freshly filled with fat, juicy flies.

"Today, we will study insects and their place in our world. To add insight to the lesson, we have a special guest. He's right outside, ready to come in." She tiptoed to the door, opened it, and motioned as though she were introducing a Hollywood star. Abram entered, smiling widely, two rectangular boxes in his hands.

"It's Abram Harsich, everyone! He's an amateur entomologist, and he's taking time from building his wonderful rainmill to lecture us. We're marvelously lucky, so *please* welcome him graciously."

She clapped lightly as Abram walked toward the front. His weight forced the hardwood floor to creak. Robert couldn't stop staring; the man attracted eyes like a magnet.

Abram set the boxes down on the desk and said, "Good morning, children."

No one answered. Robert set his teeth together, promising himself he wouldn't reply. The memory of his uncle Edmund's warning drifted through his mind. Better to be silent, to watch Abram carefully.

"Good morning," Abram repeated, his voice gentle. The words amplified inside Robert's head, became so loud he had an overpowering need to repeat them. Before he could help himself, he'd answered, "Good morning, Mr. Harsich," along with his classmates.

Abram grinned. "Mrs. Juskin has been kind enough to allow me to explain the order *Lepidoptera.*"

"We're gonna talk about leopards?" Mike Tuppence asked. Robert hadn't seen the younger boy since that day in the pool parlor. He was still wearing the same oversized shirt and suspenders.

"No, *Lepidoptera* is the name for a family of butterflies and moths. Just as dogs are called *Canis familiaris.*"

"Oh, okay," Mike said slowly. Robert could tell he didn't really understand.

"A lepidopterist catches, collects, and studies butterflies. They are the most remarkable of all Creation's creatures." Abram reached into one of the boxes, his back to the class. Robert moved from side to side, but he couldn't see what Abram was doing. The rest of the students craned their necks.

Abram turned and held his right hand high. An orange monarch butterfly sat on his gloved palm, fanning its wings. It was the largest Robert had ever seen, and its golden colors shimmered in the dullness of the room. Thirty in a jar would light the way through the gloomiest night. Robert remembered reading that it was called the monarch because it was the king of butterflies.

"A butterfly's color is in the scales of its wings." Abram's soothing voice drifted easily through the silent room. "In fact, the name *Lepidoptera* is from the Greek for 'scaly wings.'"

Robert listened intently. Mrs. Juskin had once said that Greek, Viking, and Latin words were mixed together to make the English language.

Abram brushed a finger across the tip of the monarch's closed wings. Again, Robert wondered why he was wearing gloves. Perhaps he had soft hands that blistered easily.

"If you rub off the scales, the wings become transparent as a fly's."

Abram gently raised his hand, and the butterfly floated up and skimmed above the students' heads. He laughed, and Mrs. Juskin giggled sharply. It was obvious she wanted to impress Abram.

"Butterflies live in every corner of the world," he explained. Then he lifted the lid of the box again and two more butterflies joined their brother, one light green, the other red as fire. They fluttered in circles, playing near the ceiling. If they could laugh, Robert thought, they would be laughing now.

"Colonial Americans were convinced that butterflies were beautiful witches who changed to this shape to steal butter. The Blackfoot believed that butterflies brought dreams to sleeping people. And the medieval Europeans thought they carried souls." Abram spread his fingers and the butterflies landed gently in his palms. He lowered them into the box.

"An interesting trick, eh?" he said. "Taught to me by a Goajiro of Colombia, a native shaman." He showed the class his empty hand. "I put nectar in the palm of my glove and they smelled it with their antennae."

He removed the lid from the larger box now. A blue light glowed inside. He reached in, whispering and coaxing softly. Then he brought out a giant blue butterfly, holding it in both palms. Its wingspan was at least a foot. The wings opened and closed. Robert was sure he felt a slight breeze.

"I have to be very careful with Queen Alexandra's Birdwing. That's *Ornithoptera alexandrae* if you're keeping track of proper names. This is Kachina. She is from a distant place, maybe even another world where she ruled over the butterfly kingdom for a thousand years. She once whispered her name to me in the deepest heart of a New Guinea rain forest. It will echo there forever."

Kachina lifted her wings and slowly pushed herself into the air. The eyes of the students followed her smooth, graceful flight. Time seemed to slow down. She glided over the classroom, her wings wide, a trail of glittering blue dust drifting down from her onto all the children. She glowed so brightly that a picture of her burnt in the back of Robert's mind. He thought he might never again see anything as beautiful. Tears welled in his eyes.

Then Kachina, the queen, landed gently on Abram's palms and was lowered into her box. Each child sighed sadly.

"Don't be too shy to ask me a question, anytime. If you see me downtown, pull on my shirt and say, 'Hey, Mr. Harsich, why do butter-flies have spots?' I'll answer, 'Because they look like eyes and frighten birds.' Or maybe you'll ask why they don't make noise, and I'll say, 'Butterflies used to sing, but birds said it was unfair that they were beautiful *and* could sing, so the Creator silenced the butterflies.'"

Abram grinned, looking from child to child. "That last one is a myth. A story. A legend told from man to child for generations. But there might be truth in it somewhere. Please, never hesitate to ask me anything."

He packed up his boxes and strode toward the door. Mrs. Juskin jerked to life, clapping her hands. The students applauded. Robert joined in, unable to stop himself. Abram turned, bowed, and left.

At recess, the pupils stood outside, staring north past the ele-vators, toward the rainmill, unmoving. The warm wind teased their hair. Robert joined them, breathing slowly. No one spoke about what they had seen, and he was glad. He just wanted to stand there, dreaming on his feet. When recess was over, Mrs. Juskin marched them all back into the school and had them work on addition and subtraction.

Later Robert rode home with the Vaganskis, their neighbors. The trip in the wagon was a blur, rocking him deeper into the trance. Susan Vaganski, who was three years younger, usually chat-tered all the way back—talking about her dogs, her kittens, or dresses in the Eaton's catalog—but today she remained silent, her eyes vacant. Once home, Robert mumbled, "Thanks," to Mr. Vaganski and plodded into the house. He helped with the chores, then sat down at the table.

"That mill ain't really big yet," Robert's dad said. "But it's going to be quite a fancy tower. All sorts of gadgets going in there. That Harsich knows a thing or two and he'll get it done, that's for sure."

"Is there enough food?" Robert's mother asked. The ladies in Horshoe took turns cooking for the men. "It's hard work; you need solid food."

"The pies aren't as delicious as the ones you cook, dear," Robert's dad said, patting his wife's hand. "But the stuff they give us sticks to the ribs. And the lemonade is great." He sipped his coffee. "I tell you, those blood bricks are heavy. My back aches thinking about them."

"I don't like the name," Robert's mom said.

"The name fits. They're red as red can be, and made of clay that Harsich found in the hills. He bakes them in a big old oven. They're solid as rock, fit tight together. We work like ants, carrying three times our weight."

Robert had rarely heard his dad go on so long about one subject. He did want to argue with him, though: He was sure ants carried *ten* times their weight, but he felt too sluggish to open his mouth.

"Apparently there are special gears being sent from eastern Europe," his dad continued. "That's what'll run the whole show. Though he might be able to do a test without them."

This all would have been very interesting to Robert, but a whirring, like the thrumming of distant machinery, drowned out his father's words. Robert reached for the salt, tipped it over. He looked up slowly, expecting a reprimand. His mother laughed, said something he didn't hear. He nodded, though, because it had seemed like a question. His parents continued talking to each other, their words now an indecipherable buzzing. Robert blinked several times, finding it hard to focus on the strips of bacon. It took ages to finish his meal.

He went to bed shortly after supper. When he closed his eyes, Kachina, in all her bright blue glory, still hovered before him. She floated closer, as if he were a large flower she was about to perch upon, her wings wafting a comforting breeze across his cheeks. When he opened his eyes, she vanished. He closed them and she returned. It was better to keep them closed, he decided finally.

He drifted into sleep and she flitted through his dreams. She sang softly, wanting him to get up and walk outside. To follow her. There was a new world to show him. A place of beauty and warmth, where his every dream would come true. He stirred, nearly slid himself out of bed, knocking the book beneath his pillow onto the floor.

He groggily opened his eyes. Kachina was gone. Too bad. She had seemed so real. He wrapped the blankets tight and slept. Kachina returned, continuing to call, but he was too tired to move. Her voice faded only when the morning light filtered through his window, burning his dreams away.

# CHAPTER SIXTEEN

Mrs. Juskin pulled on the string that dangled above the chalkboard, unrolling the world. Robert loved watching the map unfurl. It had been used in their schoolroom for years, but the colors of the different countries remained bright.

Robert found the green of France, where his uncles Edmund and Alden had gone during the Great War and helped to capture Vimy Ridge. That was an important name. He could tell by the way people said it, seriously, with reverence. Italy was pink, where the Romans had marched their legions. Greece, light blue, where Thermopylae was located. If he could travel to these places by merely touching a spot on the map, it would be marvelous.

Mrs. Juskin placed her pointer on the map and the class chanted, "England." Where the king comes from, Robert thought. "United States." Cowboys. "Germany." Where the Huns were. "Egypt." Land of the pyramids and the Sphinx. "China." The country of emperors.

There was a knock. Frustration wrinkling her brow, Mrs. Juskin stomped between the rows, brandishing her pointer as though she were about to fend off a dragon. The pupils watched as she opened the door.

There, framed by the doorway, stood Sergeant Ramsden in his

blue-gray uniform, hat in hand. Robert felt a sudden sense of relief: The sergeant was a hero, and he was here to help. Except his face looked tired and stony. Ramsden invited Mrs. Juskin into the cloakroom. He closed the door behind her.

Total silence descended on the class. Two desks were empty today. It wasn't unusual for some of the older kids to stay home to help harvest, but these absentees were from the rows where grades one and two sat. Robert swallowed, tried hard to remember who had sat there, but failed.

He pictured everyone's ears growing as large as a bat's, aimed at the door. The sergeant's voice, low and deep, was followed by the sharp twang of Mrs. Juskin's asking a question. Ramsden answered with one word and she moaned in response. Robert held his breath. There was a long, long silence. Then the sergeant gruffly commanded, loudly enough for them to hear, "Pull yourself together, Mrs. Juskin. The kids need you to be strong."

A decade passed. An eon. Finally the door creaked open and Sergeant Ramsden came in. Everyone faced the front, watching from the corners of their eyes. Mrs. Juskin trailed behind Ramsden like a leaf caught in an eddy of wind. Her face was red and puffy.

They stopped at the front of the classroom. Sergeant Ramsden looked at Mrs. Juskin in expectation. She slowly raised her head. "Class," she announced in a crackly voice, "this is—well, you all know Sergeant Ramsden. He has bad news and he wants your help. Please listen carefully."

Sergeant Ramsden scanned the students' faces. His gaze rested momentarily on Robert. The sergeant's jaw muscles tightened.

"I don't want to upset you," he began, "but two of your classmates have disappeared: Michael Tuppence and Susan Vaganski. They may just be skipping school, but we need to know for sure. They could be playing a trick, but this is a bad trick, because it gets the whole town upset. We're hoping one of you has seen them recently. If you know anything, please tell me now."

This was greeted with silence. The sergeant cleared his throat.

"When was the last time you saw Michael or Susan?"

Rows of clay faces said nothing. Robert's eyes darted around. It was as if they'd been turned to stone by Medusa. He tried to speak himself, but his tongue wouldn't move. Finally he spat out, "I rode home with the Vaganskis yesterday. Susan was there."

"That's right," the sergeant said. "She went home last night. Has anyone seen her since?"

Margaret Haupt's hand shot up as though it had been yanked by a string. "I saw Mike catch a ride home with his dad after school yesterday. In their wagon."

"Yes," Sergeant Ramsden said. "Good. We know he arrived home last night, too. His dad fed him supper and he went to bed early. Michael—Mike said he was very tired. Did he drop by anyone's house this morning? Was he out playing when you came to school? Was Susan?"

The students, including Robert, shook their heads. He felt odd, as though a hand were squeezing his head from above and slowly turning it back and forth. His heart thumped hard inside his chest.

The sergeant was silent. Brooding. "Do you know where these two liked to play? Did they have a favorite gully? A wood fort? Some old coyote den in the sandhills?"

Again Margaret's hand shot up. "Mike had a fort in a buffalo wallow. We all played Kill the Huns there. I was a nurse. Bobby lost his leg—well, not really, but I bandaged him up."

"Good. Good. Maybe we can check it out."

"It's near our farm. A fort made of branches and broken boards. It's easy to see 'cause there's a flag. Well, red underpants." She giggled.

"Anything else?" Sergeant Ramsden asked.

Robert wanted to mention the butterflies, but there was a will—a force—holding him back. He fought against it and said, "Maybe they followed the butterfly's singing."

"What do you mean?"

"I dreamed about a butterfly," he explained. He struggled to find words that would make the sergeant understand that this wasn't just *any* butterfly. "Sh-she wanted me to fly with her."

"I did too," Margaret said, then clamped her mouth shut.

"And me," a third boy admitted. "The queen of butterflies."

Ramsden crossed his arms. "Butterflies? I don't understand."

Mrs. Juskin, who was leaning against her desk, said, "Abram Harsich showed butterflies to the students yesterday as part of our science class. They were amazingly beautiful. Obviously the children were affected by it."

"I see." Ramsden nodded. His brow was still furrowed. He cleared his throat. "Well, if anyone hears or sees anything of these two kids, you tell me, okay?"

He thanked Mrs. Juskin and left, his heavy boots clunking on the hardwood floor. The students watched him go. Mrs. Juskin plopped herself into her seat and sighed sadly. She hid her face in her hands, seemed to be weeping.

"Just open your readers to any page and start reading." Her voice cracked. "We'll begin your lessons later. Right now I need a little break."

# CHAPTER SEVENTEEN

ROBERT PUSHED A DUMPLING THROUGH THE GRAVY ON HIS PLATE, pretending the white lump was a dreadnought cutting through the ocean.

"Don't play with your food," his mother said.

He lowered his fork to the plate, dropped his hands to his sides.

The front door swung open and his father strode in, arms reddened with clay, plaid shirt partly unbuttoned and stained with sweat.

"You're dirty as sin," his mom said, getting up to peck his dad's cheek. Robert cringed. They never used to kiss so much in front of him.

"I'll wash up," his dad chirped. "Cleanliness is next to godliness." He winked at Robert, went to the back room, and within a few minutes was seated at the head of the table. Clean and godly.

"Chicken!" he said. "I told the boys we'd be having chicken."

Robert's mother took her seat and his dad quickly said grace. The words made Robert drool in anticipation. He cut into his chicken, finding the meat moist. He stabbed a piece, brought it to his mouth, and chewed thoughtfully. This was expensive chicken from the butcher's. His mom had bought it a few days before. The price didn't seem to bother his parents. They were so sure they'd be making lots of money by the next fall.

Chickens. Ham. Money. Rain. It all sounded so beautiful to Robert. Like . . . like Eden. He had heard at school that a family from Maple Creek was so poor they'd had to eat their pet pony. And here he was chomping on chicken. Nearly every night.

His mom had given him two spoonfuls of peas, so he speared a few. They were green and perfectly round. Tiny planets exploding with taste. He tried a steamed carrot. It dripped with butter. Nothing was burnt or bad tasting. He could paint a picture of this meal and it would hang in a gallery forever: the best dinner ever made.

"Abram's pleased with everything!" Robert's dad blurted out, and two peas shot out of his mouth, tumbled across the table. He looked sheepishly at his wife, who grinned. They both giggled. "Sorry about that cannon shot. Just having too much fun." He wiped his lips. "Did I tell you, son, how hard we work there? It's like we're a bunch of ants carrying three times our weight."

Robert swallowed a chewed-up piece of chicken. His dad had already spoken about this once before. "Ants carry *ten* times their weight," Robert pointed out.

"Oh, sorry, son. It *feels* like ten times our weight."

"When will they try the rainmill out?" his mom asked. She was at the counter whipping cream. It seemed she never sat through a whole meal; she went from task to task, hovering briefly over her food to peck at it like a bird.

"Maybe Sunday. Abram says he wants to do a test run before it gets cold."

Robert was hypnotized by the circular motion of his mother's arm. Round and round the bowl, waiting for the cream to thicken, stopping only to add more sugar. The last rays of the setting sun shone through the window, painting the counter red.

"Two kids disappeared today," Robert said quietly.

His mom kept whipping. His father chewed thoughtfully.

Robert felt his lips. They were numb. Had his parents not heard? He sliced into the soft white flesh of a dumpling with his fork, like cutting into a cloud. He placed it in his mouth and chewed. It was perfectly salted. He added more salt to see if he could make it taste bad. He tried it—as good as the bite before. He moved the dumplings to the side of his plate.

"Two kids vanished today." He raised his voice this time. "A boy and a girl from school."

"What?" Robert's dad blinked, and he looked surprised, as though Robert had just now suddenly appeared in his seat. "What did you say?"

"Sergeant Ramsden came to school. He told us Mike Tuppence and Susan Vaganski are missing."

"They're probably out wandering around somewhere," Robert's mom said. "Mr. Tuppence doesn't keep a good eye on his boy, and the Vaganskis, they're wonderful neighbors, but Clara just doesn't understand how to discipline her children. All seven of them are wild brats. But don't worry. Little boys and girls wander all the time. No harm ever happens. They go away, then come back. They always come back."

His mom went back to whipping the cream. His father cut up his last piece of chicken.

Robert thought for a moment. "Maybe they're gone forever. Like Matthew."

"Matthew's not gone," she said, casually tasting the whipped cream, "he's . . . out for a while. He'll be back."

"Your mother's right." Robert's dad spoke slowly, as though he were talking to a three-year-old. "Your brother is visiting someone. Your grandma in Moose Jaw. That's who he's staying with. She'll bring him back in the spring."

Robert blinked back tears. "He's dead, like a baby sparrow fallen out of the nest."

"He's not dead," his mom whispered. She brought Robert a plate of chocolate cake and whipped cream. A thin smile curled across her lips. "Don't mention it again, dear. Just eat up and don't mention it again."

# CHAPTER EIGHTEEN

**R**OBERT STOOD AT THE EDGE OF ABRAM HARSICH'S FARMYARD, AND the sun behind him in the west stretched his shadow to twelve times his height. He moved his shadow hand and grabbed his dad's elbow fifty feet away, then squeezed Mrs. Samuelson's meaty leg. He tapped Mr. Ruggles on the shoulder. Hello, shopkeeper, how're the vegetables today?

Abram had invited a crowd to celebrate the first test of the rainmill. It was Sunday, and most everyone from town and the surrounding farms was there, dressed in their finest clothes, bearing baskets full of bread, vegetables, jams, meats, cheese, and pies. Robert had eaten so much his stomach bulged out. He wondered if it would explode, his intestines unraveling like ropes.

The rainmill loomed above them like a watchtower. He guessed it was at least sixty feet high. The first thirty feet or so was a cylinder of red clay bricks. Then twenty feet of metal girding sat on top of that, framing a series of pulleys and gears. Four gunmetal-gray vanes creaked in the breeze, waiting to be released. At the highest point were several lightning rods, twisted like snakes.

Mr. Samuelson, clad in his tuxedo, stood on a platform decorated with red banners. He leaned on the podium. A cigar was lodged between his fingers and he waved it as he barked loudly about interest rates on loans and investments in a series of rainmills. Boring, dull, loud words. Robert yawned and stretched his shadow hand out, trying to flick the cigar from Samuelson's grasp.

Some of the women clutched umbrellas, as though expecting to beat a thief away. Robert had seen umbrellas only twice: in the Eaton's catalog, and when it had rained on a Sunday three years ago and several ladies had brought them to church. His mother wanted one, but there had never been enough rain to justify the purchase.

He could yank the umbrellas out of their arms with his shadow hands. Or pinch the rears of the old widows. He reached up, pinched Mrs. Torence's wide buttocks, and chuckled. Take that! He pinched again, felt guilty for a moment, then gave Mrs. Juskin's buttocks a twisting squeeze. Ha! Fat bums, pinching their fat bums! He guffawed. Mrs. Juskin glanced back, and Robert quickly dropped his arms and examined an imaginary bird in the sky.

People wandered around. Samuelson had finished his speech, but nothing followed. Robert wondered if there was something wrong with the rainmill. Several of the men were tightening bolts and testing pulleys. All the other boys and girls stood next to their parents.

Robert skipped away, his shadow dancing behind him. In the cool shade cast by the Harsich house, he found himself drawn to the windows. He knew it was wrong to peek inside, but he couldn't help it. Maybe Kachina would be there, circling the house like a pet bird. He pressed his nose against the glass. Light flooded in from the opposite window, revealing a small square table and three heavy wooden chairs. No pictures or calendars hung on the wall. The only objects he saw were a washbasin, a gray mug, and a vase on the counter.

Robert glanced back at the crowd. His mom and dad were talking to Mrs. Samuelson. He sneaked along the side of the house to a small round window that reminded him of a ship's porthole. He stood on his tippy-toes, stretching his frame as far as he could, digging his fingers into the sill. Up, up, peeking in.

A flash of pink. Of yellow. And green.

Butterflies! Several of them glided around the room. Vines wove up and down the wall, flowers in full bloom across every inch. Droplets of moisture dotted the window. The sight made his eyes shoot back and forth, trying to take it all in. His spine ached as he stretched higher and higher. The butterflies should have gone south, yet here they were.

*Fecund.* It meant green and growing; his uncle had used the word once. It was a word adults and teachers might know, but he had kept it in his head. How had Abram gotten the green of Eden inside this room?

Then, like a descending blue angel, Kachina appeared, her majestic wings moving slowly as she floated down to the windowsill, just inches away. Her eyes were ebony ovals, and one of her six legs was held up, as in a salute. The very picture of her would be tattooed forever on the inside of his eyelids.

"She really is a beautiful creature," a familiar voice said.

Robert shuddered and let go of the sill. Turning, he lost his balance and leaned against the house.

"I'm sorry, I . . . I . . ."

"It's all right." Abram was smiling. In the shade he looked twice as pale. "Even an old lepidopterist like me still watches Kachina with wonder. She's worth standing on your tiptoes for." He put a gloved hand to his chin, as though he was thinking hard. "You intrigue me, Robert."

Robert looked up at Abram's thin features: the nose straight as a metal rod, the eyes that glowed slightly red. They were focused on Robert now, a penetrating gaze. "You love the butterfly queen, don't you?" Robert nodded. "Have you ever dreamed about her?"

He wanted to lie, but instead whispered, "Yes." It felt good to tell the truth, to share this secret. Yes, he had dreamed about her. Yes, he loved Kachina! He thought about her every day.

"You are on the cusp," Abram explained, "between boy and man, the dreaming and the reality. You must have had a million great dreams in your lifetime. Of armies and swords, candies and milkwhips, wizards and unicorns. The cusp." His lips curled into a soft, sad smile. "I have never had a dream. Not once." He leaned against the wall. "Do you know what dust is, boy?"

"Dry dirt," Robert said.

Abram laughed softly. "Yes, that's true. It's soil without enough moisture to bind it together." He scooped a handful of dirt from a bank that had formed beside his house. He let it fall between his gloved fingers. "'I'll give you as many years of life as grains of sand squeezed in your hand.' A Greek god once promised that in a myth. I heard the myth when it was first spoken around a fire near Athens. But I have had many more years than a fistful of sand. Many more. All because of dust."

Robert was nervous. He sensed that he was about to be pinned against the wall, an eleven-year-old human trophy to be displayed along with Abram's butterflies. Abram leaned toward him, and Robert cowered.

"Have you ever caught a moth and gently rubbed its wings? You get dust on your hands. The dust is the magic that gives it flight." Abram began peeling his right glove off. Robert was hypnotized, watching to see what lay underneath. "Not all dust is inanimate, you know. Some say there is a special living dust around us in the shape of wings. Our souls, perhaps. In every color imaginable. Children have vast quantities of this dust, but gathering it is a very tricky process."

The glove was off, revealing mottled skin. Abram reached toward Robert with his naked hand. His fingers were mummified, slender as twigs. Robert couldn't budge; his boots were glued to the ground. He desperately wanted to shout or crouch down, but he'd become a statue. He focused on Abram's ancient, rotted fingers, the nails cracked.

"This dust, this commodity, is valuable," Abram whispered as he touched Robert's forehead with cold, rough fingertips. Robert's skull grew numb. "It's worth more than rubies and emeralds. If you harvest and refine it, you can make yourself immortal. Or use it to mesmerize minds. Get men and women to forget their cares." Robert felt as if the fingers were going deeper into his head, grasping an essential part of him, tugging at it. No, he thought. You can't have me.

Abram yanked away his hand as though it had been burnt. His smile didn't falter. Robert blinked, pulled back.

"You *are* wily," Abram said. "No matter. Others weren't. They have become . . . merchandise. And to find the right, how shall I put it—traders?—for such goods, you have to search far, send messages out to the stars." He pointed skyward with his bonelike fingers. "These traders, they— Well, even your mind couldn't imagine them. They exist in another place—a place that's cold and empty. It's right next to us. Around us." His eyes flashed red. "Simple to find it, really, if you've trained for centuries." He traced an S shape in the air, then cupped his hands together and blew softly between his thumbs. "See? Look on my works, ye Mighty." He chuckled as he uncupped his hands to reveal an insect. "With the flick of a wrist I have brought you a locust."

Robert stared. The creature was large, nearly the length of Abram's finger, its round eyes dark as pools of cave water. Its antennae whipped back and forth as though searching for food, its mandibles opening and closing. "If I released him, there would suddenly be a hundred, a thousand, a hundred thousand locusts devouring the crops. Just a twitch of my fingers and your parents would starve; this land would die forever." The locust tested its wings: *chir-chir-chir.* "This creature is from that other place and it has an endless hunger." He caressed the locust and it lifted its back legs, scratching itself against his finger. Without a pause, Abram closed his fist and squished it. A yellowish white substance leaked between his fingers and dripped to the ground. Then he slowly slipped on his glove. "I'm just a locust to these traders. They have the real power. But they will come bearing gifts of splendor. Maybe even rain. They want the living dust in its purest form and they will trade anything for it—even a soul of your own, cut to perfect size. Can you imagine that, Robert? I've done everything a man could wish to do, but I've never closed my eyes and dreamed. Or felt love. You need a soul for that." He paused, wetted his lips with his ivory tongue. "Your brother understood."

Robert narrowed his eyes. "So *you* took Matthew! Where is he? Did you hurt him? Did . . . did you take his dust?"

This time Abram's smile showed white, perfect teeth. "I've never hurt anyone. And Matthew is still here." He gestured around him. "We're all still here today."

Robert tightened his fists. He wanted to point at Abram. To shout. But his lips wouldn't move. All he could do was shake with anger.

"I've spoken too much," Abram said. "Upset you. I am an old,

old man. You'll forget in a few months that we've exchanged pleasantries. Hair will sprout on your body. Muscles will grow stronger. Your thoughts will become . . . more adult. But it's been good, for now, to talk to someone who believes me." He dismissed Robert with a wave of his hand. "Run along and join your parents. The show is about to begin."

Robert didn't run. He walked, slowly, toward the podium. He was dying to glance at Abram; he could feel Abram staring at the back of his skull, laughing. He willed himself to look straight ahead, but after a few more yards he turned. Abram was gone.

Robert gawked at the stage just as Abram strode to the podium, sleeves rolled to his elbows as though he were about to pitch hay. How had he gotten there so quickly? He waited for the crowd to settle down.

"It's here," he said, and his words were perfectly clear to Robert. "We have built it." Abram pointed at the rainmill. "It's not perfect yet. There are special gears and locumocuters and other technical items I've ordered from Europe that may not arrive for months. But it will work well enough for now."

He raised one hand, palm up. "I was going to give a long, boring speech today, but actions speak louder than words."

He nodded to Samuelson, who motioned to someone else standing inside the rainmill. A sound like timber snapping in two was followed by the humming of a hundred thousand bumblebees. Light flashed inside the mill. Two glass batteries, which sat in a cubbyhole halfway up the tower, crackled with electricity. The giant vanes on the rainmill turned, and the crowd gasped.

The vanes spun as fast as an airplane propeller. Robert wondered if the rainmill would lift off. For several minutes the humming and crackling continued, but nothing else happened. Then, just as the crowd began to mumble, someone pointed to the east.

A dark flicker of a cloud appeared on the horizon. Robert squinted. The cloud seemed to be spooling out of a hole in the sky. Behind it were ghostly shapes, moving like tentacles or hands, as though they were working on a loom. Robert blinked. No, he was mistaken—they were just other wisps of darker cloud. The hole closed, and the cloud skittered toward them like a trout caught on a hook, fighting all the way. It wasn't big, not like the hail clouds Robert had seen, but it was the same color.

In no time it was above them, larger now, blocking out the sun, and hovering and spinning so close it seemed he could jump up and touch it. It thundered once, shaking every bone in his body; then it attacked the rainmill with several bolts of lightning. And still the vanes spun.

Finally, as though in surrender, the cloud gave up its rain. The drops fell gently from the sky, sunlight turning them into watery diamonds.

At first everyone sighed and shouted in awe; then the rain sluiced down, and the umbrellas the women were holding popped open. The dust at their feet turned to mud. People laughed and gathered, three or four under each umbrella. Full-grown men opened their mouths to catch the rain. Robert's parents gazed at the heavens with smiles on their faces. Robert couldn't help thinking about the hippopotamuses his father had always joked about—it was going to be wet enough that they could move here.

He opened his mouth. The rain tasted of sugar. He caught more droplets on his tongue. So sweet. Not dirty like the rain he remembered. Uncle Alden had once told him that every drop of rain had a piece of dirt in it, but these drops didn't.

He spat, barely missing Mrs. Juskin's leg. Rain shouldn't taste like sugar. He knew it was wrong. He spat again.

The rainmill slowed, and the cloud dispersed into smaller pieces of black cotton until there was nothing left. The sun, now at the edge of the horizon, shot a blast of heat at the people of Horshoe, as though it had grown angry at this brief interruption in its reign. It dried the farmers' hair, warmed the ground until the puddles disappeared and all they were left with was mud stains on their clothes and boots. The vanes spun more and more slowly, and Abram looked down at them all, his bloodless lips curled into a crescent-shaped smile.

# CHAPTER NINETEEN

THE MONTHS WENT BY QUICKLY. THE EARTH GREW HARD AND COLD. Hoarfrost coated the fallow fields with glittering, icy diamonds, outlining spiderwebs between the strands of stubble. Winter brought several inches of snow, but a strong wind excavated the dust, painting the banks brown.

Robert lowered a wax angel onto the windowsill and straightened the wick. He set another angel beside her. Half her head had been melted last year, scarring her face. He pried the wick from the wax, whispering, "This'll be your last Christmas. Burn brightly!"

His mother was hanging the stockings over the fireplace, humming carols.

It was dark and cold outside the window, and his fingers grew slightly numb with the chill. December was nearly over; Christmas would arrive tomorrow. He put the third angel in place, wishing he were more excited. Last year he'd been counting every minute. This year, the anticipation had already worn off. I'm getting older, he thought, fear tingling in his stomach. I don't want to get older if this is what happens.

A week ago he'd gone with his father to find a pine in the Cypress Hills, brought back a dandy one, and helped to decorate it. His mom and dad had put four presents under the branches, and all four were for him, two more than last year. He had been thrilled. He'd lifted them, had tried to peek through the corners of the wrapping, had shaken them, then stopped. There wasn't a present for Matthew.

He hadn't touched the presents since.

Robert turned to ask his mother what to do next, then froze. She had hung three red stockings above the fireplace and was about to put up the fourth. Was she remembering Matthew? Or were her memories still buried under promises of rain and good crops? Buried by false dreams.

She looked over at the picture of Edmund, nodded toward it as though they were having a conversation. Robert's heart rate doubled. Had Edmund blinked at her? Waved? She turned away from the photograph and attempted to fasten the fourth and smallest stocking to a nail, but it slipped. She tried again, but the lace wouldn't hold. She frowned, shook her head slowly, then lowered the stocking into the wooden box where all the Christmas ornaments were kept.

Robert sighed. He understood. He had his own struggle: Days would pass without his thinking about his brother. There was a photograph on the mantel of the whole family in their good clothes, but even there Matthew seemed faded and unfamiliar, almost like a stranger—a little boy who'd stumbled into the wrong picture.

"Will you light the candles, son?" his mother asked. She was carrying the box to the storage closet. "Uncle Alden will appreciate seeing a light in the window."

Robert found the matchbox by the fireplace and went back to the angels. He opened the box, fumbled with a wooden match, and struck it against the side of the box. The match head burst into flame, and the sulfur stung his nose. He loved that scent. He lit each angel, then watched the match burn.

Robert struggled to remember that he'd wanted to talk with Uncle Alden. To tell him about Matthew and Abram, and the dust. Uncle Alden was the only one who would understand. Robert had it figured out, at least partly. But it was getting harder to keep that knowledge in his head. He would remember only when he was reading his Jules Verne book.

He waited until the match burned down to his fingers, then blew it out.

Within an hour his dad came in from chores and his uncle arrived, clutching three shoddily wrapped presents. They had a turkey dinner, with potatoes, thick gravy, and peas. His parents chattered the whole time, and Uncle Alden smiled and nodded. He looked thinner, almost as if he were starting to disappear. He was the first to go back for seconds. When he went up for thirds, Robert's mom said, "That'll fatten you up for one of those widows." Uncle Alden turned to Robert and said, "I think your parents are getting simple in their old age." They laughed. Robert pretended to chuckle along.

After an apple pie dessert, they retired to the living room.

There the prattle continued until Robert's dad excused himself, saying, "I hear the outhouse calling me. It's gonna be a chilly visit." Robert's mom went into the kitchen to make another pot of coffee.

Uncle Alden sat in a wicker rocking chair, smoking a pipe and rocking back and forth next to the fireplace. He blew a perfect smoke ring and winked at Robert. "If I could get paid for making those, I'd be a rich man. Truth be told, though, I'd be happy to be paid for anything these days."

Robert nodded. He knew he didn't have much time. "I think Abram Harsich took Matthew," he spluttered. "He hid him some-where."

His uncle stopped rocking. "Hold on." He pointed the pipe at Robert. "What in blue blazes are you talking about? Abram's a snake, but that's a serious allegation. What makes you say it?"

"He . . . he collects dust. From little boys and girls, and from the wings of butterflies, I think—it's like—it's their souls, and he uses it." The words were getting jumbled up in his head; when he'd rehearsed this speech he'd sounded as certain as a judge laying down a law. "That's how Abram made the mirror in the theater work. And I think it's how the rainmill turns. And he's got this room with butterflies in it. It's all green and perfect. But it's wrong. Every-thing's wrong. You see, he doesn't have a soul."

Uncle Alden narrowed his eyes, a serious look on his face. "You're pretty upset, aren't you?"

"Yes," Robert answered.

His uncle smiled, sucked in smoke, blew out a gray, wispy ring. "Well, don't go getting your long johns in a knot. Dust? Souls powering mirrors? How old are you now?"

"Eleven."

"Well, you know better than to go making things up. Where'd you get such ideas?"

Robert was silent. The dishes had stopped clinking together in the kitchen. Was his mom listening?

"Well?" his uncle asked.

Robert's mother dropped a spoon or something on the floor.

"Abram cornered me when they tested the mill. Told me about the dust. And said he took Matthew."

"He *said* that?"

Robert strained to remember the exact words. "No. Just that Matthew was still there."

"At his farm?"

"I don't know. I was . . . frightened."

Uncle Alden took another puff, thinking hard. Smoke leaked out of his nostrils and lips, as if a coal fire were burning inside his head. "I can't see it."

"It's true."

"He's wicked, but to steal a child he'd have to be crazy. Abram isn't crazy; he just has a crazy plan. He's a snake-oil salesman. That's all. I think he was playing games with you." Uncle Alden narrowed his eyes. "Do you know what *mesmerize* means?"

Robert nodded. "To hypnotize."

"More than a hundred years ago there was a man in Paris called Franz Anton Mesmer. He believed he had magnetic powers. He would mentally compel groups of people to dance, sleep, sing, or fall on the floor and convulse. He thought he was healing them. They had no control over their actions." Uncle Alden pointed his pipe again. "That's what Abram is. Probably one of the best mesmerists on the continent. He's used his powers of magnetism to get everyone to build this tower of Babel."

Babel. Robert recognized that from the Bible. It had to do with why people spoke different languages; a big tower that had made God angry.

Uncle Alden continued. "It's mass hypnotism. A combination of sounds and spinning lights. I think it first happened in the theater. A trick on the brain. That's why everyone's forgetting things. He's planted hypnotic suggestions in people's heads. You say *rainmill* and they get all enthusiastic and run off at the mouth about how great it is. How great Abram is. How everything's coming up petunias. Day or night, there's always a talkie playing at the film theater. He wants to keep everyone occupied. You hear the train lately?"

"Train?" Robert asked. "What train?"

"Came through town about noon the other day. Gave a big, long, mournful toot on its horn. I'm standing in Ruggles's store and damned if Ruggles doesn't set his head down on the counter and take a nap, right there. I got tired as the dickens, too. Go outside and no one's about. Just Old Man Spooky, drunk as a skunk, whimpering on a bench. Poor sot."

"I don't understand," Robert said.

"The train's horn is another hypnotic suggestion. Sends the people deeper into a trance. I'm waiting patiently, Robert, because come spring that rainmill won't be worth the brick it's piled on. It won't work. The spell will break and he'll be run out of town faster than you can say *conniving con man*." He took another pull at his pipe, then immediately sucked in again. He examined the tobacco and discovered that it had gone out.

"Do you still have dreams?" Robert asked.

Uncle Alden emptied the tobacco into a clay bowl. "Of course. Everyone does. The mind moving its garbage around. Why?"

"What did you see in the mirror?"

"We talked about this. I've thought it over. I saw clouds. That's what Abram wanted me to see, Lord knows why. Your eyes can be fooled. Ever wonder why the moon is bigger some nights? It's a trick the light plays. That's all that happened in the theater."

Robert sat back. He understood now that he would find no ally in his uncle. Abram's words returned: *You are on the cusp. Between the dreaming and the reality.*

Uncle Alden could write stories and read books, but he was past the cusp. Too old to believe in magic and soul dust. An adult.

Robert hardly slept at all on Christmas Eve.

# CHAPTER TWENTY

ON THE FIRST DAY ROBERT FELT WINTER RELEASE ITS COLD, COLD claws from the land, it rained. He and his parents ran outside and stood in the downpour. They were laughing, but Robert caught a few drops on his tongue. They tasted sugary. It wasn't real rain, he was sure of it. He retreated to the doorway and watched his parents jumping in the gathering puddles; then he slipped inside the house, went up to his room, and read.

The rain didn't stop for several days.

The people of Horshoe came together on the sixth straight day of rain and had an impromptu dance at the town hall, musicians bringing their guitars and fiddles, stomping their boots to a steady beat. It wasn't raining anywhere else: Maple Creek hadn't had a drop, Swift Current was as dry as a buffalo bone. But in Horshoe it was a jungle. A rain forest, Robert thought. No, a rain prairie. Soon the countryside would be as thick with green vegetation as the strange room in Abram's house.

Robert's parents took him to the dance and found a table near the front of the hall. His mother sat, looking stern, but her foot tapped to the music. She once playfully shook her finger at a drunken man who staggered over to their table. Robert's dad laughed.

Some of the men, crazy with fever or joy, scrambled outside, dove into puddles, then returned looking like muddy savages, hooting and dancing, stopping only to drink rye whiskey. Dermot McFaden, the butcher, had a half-grown pig squirming under his arm. He'd give it a drink from a bottle of hooch, then hand the bottle to the nearest man, who'd take a swig and squeal like a hog.

Abram Harsich watched from a table on the stage, the banker beside him. At one point, when the music stopped, Abram raised a glass and toasted the wet sky. The town toasted him back. A few women paraded up and kissed his cheeks.

Uncle Alden plodded up to their table and sat next to Robert's dad. His hair was slick against his forehead.

"How much rain you get?" he asked.

"About six inches," Robert's dad answered. He tapped his fingers on the table.

"Not a drop has touched my land. The clouds roll on by."

Robert's dad shrugged. "Mother Nature can be funny sometimes. Rewards those who work hard. Who believe. You still think it's a snake-oil trick?"

"Doesn't seem to matter what I believe," Uncle Alden replied softly. "I'll be broke if I don't get a crop. Samuelson ain't exactly in the charity business."

"Then maybe you should sign up for a work detail. Couldn't hurt your chances, could it?"

No, Robert thought. Don't.

"I might have to," Uncle Alden said, his voice bleak. He shuffled over to the bar and returned with a bottle of beer. It wasn't long before he was up to get another.

The dance became more raucous, the music louder. Men and women twirled together wildly, sometimes hitting tables or walls. No one got hurt.

Robert noticed a square-jawed man sitting near the wall, not smiling. He looked familiar. Then Robert recognized Sergeant Ramsden in civilian clothing.

He's undercover, Robert thought. He kept waiting for the Mountie to get up, nab Abram, and drag him away, but the sergeant didn't move. Occasionally he'd talk to whoever was near him.

Abram left before midnight, his truck rumbling like thunder. The dance ended shortly afterward and everyone went home happy.

The sun came out Sunday, then disappeared behind the clouds Monday. Sun. Rain. Sun. Rain. The grass grew green, even in the Steelgate farmyard, where it hadn't been green in Robert's lifetime.

A shipment of umbrellas arrived by train and sold out within an hour. A second shipment was ordered.

Sun. Rain. Sun. Rain.

That became the pattern of everyone's lives.

# CHAPTER TWENTY·ONE

**O**N A SATURDAY IN LATE MAY, ROBERT CAME DOWN THE STAIRS dressed in his work clothes. His mother was in the kitchen; the scent of baking bread loaves filled the house, made him salivate. It would be so good to sit at the table and cut a slice from that steaming hot bread just out of the oven. He would spread butter and honey across it, then slowly chew on it, savoring every taste. Maybe there were buns, too.

He almost went into the kitchen, but stopped in the living room, gathering his will. He didn't need the bread. He'd had breakfast already. The bread was a distraction and he refused to be distracted today. He had a task.

He stared at the picture of Uncle Edmund on the mantel, hoping that his uncle would wink or move or wave. I'm ready, Robert thought. Send me a signal. A sign.

He waited. Nothing happened. It was only a photograph. Robert touched the frame, found it warm. That's odd, he thought; then he realized the sun had been shining through the window above the piano, heating the metal. He tapped the picture once for luck, then wandered outside.

It was sunny, so he rolled his sleeves up to his elbows. His mother thought he was on his way to do chores, but he walked past the barn and along the fence line. The grass was green and slippery. The dull grumbling of a tractor reverberated through the air—somewhere over a low hill, his father was seeding.

It was a special day. Robert had circled it on the calendar in his room because he had promised himself he would go for a long walk on this date.

Matthew's birthday.

Neither parent had spoken of Matthew that morning. They hadn't mentioned him since autumn. It was as if Matthew existed only in Robert's head. He's real, Robert told himself. He used to walk here. Before the rain and the grass.

Robert cut across a field planted with wheat. His father had used the tractor to drag the seeder through the soil. Last year he'd talked about going back to hiring Clydesdale horses for the work, but this year, with the loan payments deferred, he'd not once complained about the price of gas. A few green stalks had already popped through the soil. There were no weeds.

Robert was far enough from the house that his mother wouldn't see him, so he turned toward the grid road and crawled over a barbed-wire fence plugged with green Russian thistles. They had lost their hardness and wormed tentative roots into the ground.

Tumbleweeds that didn't tumble. Robert thought about that. It was unnatural.

He crossed a ditch choked with grass and headed onto the gravel road. The scent of wolf willow followed him; the shrub had sprung up along the fence line, its ghostly silver leaves glistening with dew, while bright yellow flowers caught the sun.

His skin was soft. He didn't think he'd ever get used to that feeling. His skin had always itched or peeled in the hot sun; now it was soft and brand-new. Everything felt brand-new. All about him the world was green and colorful. Purple crocuses were clumped together in an unseeded corner of the field. Dandelions glowed yellow on the edge of the road. The Cypress Hills were emerald green in the distance, a haze of fog slipping around their haunches.

He had decided to trace Matthew's last walk into town. Robert was forgetting bits and pieces of his brother. The more it rained, the more time passed, the older he got. Soon memories of Matthew would be gone, and there would be no marker to say he'd ever been there. Not even a gravestone.

Grasshoppers slowly crawled across the road, trying to dry their wings. They looked smaller than last year, as though the rain had shrunk them.

The distant buzz of a motor made Robert turn. A vehicle was coming down the road, with not even the slightest trace of dust behind it. The sunlight glinted off its windshield. He thought briefly about stepping into the ditch, but instead he moved to the side and kept walking. He stared ahead as the sound of the motor grew closer. The car stopped right beside him and he saw the Royal Canadian Mounted Police crest on the passenger door.

Sergeant Ramsden got out and strode over to Robert. During

the winter a gray patch had appeared in his short hair. "You need a ride?" he asked.

Robert wondered what the right answer was. Did he? Or was it better to walk?

The sergeant smiled. "Cat got your tongue?"

"Sure. Sure I need a ride," Robert said.

The sergeant opened the passenger door and Robert climbed in. The interior smelled of oil and smoke, as though a gun had gone off. Sergeant Ramsden slammed the door, but it refused to stay closed, so he pushed it into place until the bolt clicked. Then he got in on his side and started down the road.

"You out walking for any special reason?" he asked.

"Just wanted to."

"Do your parents know you're here?"

Robert briefly considered telling a lie. All he had to do was say, *Yes, they do.* But today he was looking for the truth.

"No," he said. "I wanted to be alone."

Ramsden was silent for a few seconds. "Do they ever talk about your brother?"

"No." Again the truth. "They . . . they've forgotten him, I think."

Ramsden let out his breath. "There's something awfully weird about this town. No one can recall much of anything. Do you remember your classmates who disappeared?"

"Yes." Robert paused. "Mike Tuppence and Susan Vaganski," he said. It had been very hard to find those names in his head.

"No one else does. Even their parents pretend they were

never here. Some other kids are gone too. One in Montana. Another in Alberta. Makes me wonder what this world is coming to." He shook his head. "And the land around here is all weird. Go six miles east or west and the grass stops growing and the fields are all sand, but here it's spring. Like it was when I was a kid. It's not natural." The sergeant's big hands were tight on the wheel. "That Abram guy ever come back to your school?"

"No."

"Your parents friends with him?"

"Dad worked on the rainmill."

Ramsden nodded. "Most everyone has." He didn't say anything for a time, driving down the road, scanning the green fields. Horshoe's elevators loomed in the sky. "Where do you want to go?" he asked.

"The store."

Ramsden turned down Main Street and stopped the car in front of the grocer's. Robert shouldered the door. It squeaked as it opened. Once out, he looked at the sergeant.

"You stay away from that Abram, you hear?" Ramsden warned. "He's . . . he's not who he says he is. He told me he's from the States, but he's not. I found that out."

"I will."

Robert pushed the door closed. Sergeant Ramsden set the car in motion and continued down the street.

Once the police car was gone, Horshoe remained silent. No one else was on the sidewalk, though a car and a truck were parked in front of the hotel. Not a soul could be heard or seen anywhere.

Robert walked past the laundry. The door was closed, no sign of the Chinese women. He peered through the window of Lee Yuen's restaurant, where he and Matthew had often sipped vanilla milkwhips. I'd love a milkwhip now, Robert thought. With chocolate shavings floating in the creamy foam. He licked his lips.

No one was at the tables or behind the counter. He kept walking, furtively glancing at the Royal Theatre. The stone lion glowered at him. The eerie sound of a piano slipped out from under the door. Robert quickened his pace. He didn't want to know what talkie was playing—Abram had set it up, whatever it was. It would be a trick. Robert would open the door and be gone forever.

He ambled up to the school, then over to the church. It had been months since he'd been inside God's house; it already looked unkempt. A new reverend had never arrived and no one seemed to have noticed.

Robert continued walking, veering away from the tiny brick powerhouse, afraid of the electricity that gathered there and sparked out across the town on spiderweb lines, lighting Main Street and all the houses.

On his second time through downtown, he passed by the hotel. Someone was sleeping on one of the benches, clothes dirty and ragged. Robert circled away, figuring it was Old Man Spooky, who tended to babble in his drunken stupor and was likely to reach out and grab you, calling his dead wife's name.

Spooky had grown up here, Robert remembered, had made money on the stock market, built the theater, lost everything in the crash. Then his wife had died, and now his only friend was the bottle. It was very sad. But it was also a good story. Like out of a book.

"Robert," Spooky whispered.

Robert started. The old man lifted his arm, raised his head. Robert stopped, swallowed.

It was Uncle Alden.

He looked feverish, his face marked by stubble, his eyes unfocused. His boots were caked with dried mud.

"Is that you, Robert?" he asked again, voice cracking.

"Yes." He walked over to the bench as his uncle slowly sat up. Uncle Alden ran a hand through his hair, and pieces of dirt fell out of it. He rubbed at his eyes with the back of his wrist. "I've been rained on," he said. "Man, I've been rained on hard." He gestured for Robert to sit.

Robert did so, first knocking some of the mud off the bench. "Are you sick? Do you want me to get the doctor?"

Uncle Alden grinned crazily. Even his teeth were dirty. The smile frightened Robert; it was as though his uncle had been trying to eat dirt. Even kids know not to do that, he thought.

"Sick?" His uncle echoed. "Yeah, in my head. Been walking

into town every day for the last week. Coming to sign the volunteer sheet. It's worn me out."

"Did you sign?" Robert asked quietly.

Uncle Alden rubbed his nose. "Every morning I'd have this dream with butterflies, very odd and beautiful. Then I'd start tramping to town, not even stopping to eat, thinking I really should sign up. I'd get to the bank, see the list on the wall, grab the pen, and set it to the paper. Then one thought would pop into my head: What in Sam Hades am I doing here? I'd drop the pen and walk all the way back to the farm. Do the same thing the next day. And the next. I was going to sign today. I felt it in my heart. I just couldn't fight anymore. But when I got to the bank, I caught my reflection in the window." He lowered his voice to a whisper. "But it wasn't me. It was Edmund looking back through the window. He shook his head at me like he was ashamed. It was a dream. An apparition."

"It was real," Robert said. "You know it was."

Uncle Alden stared at Robert. "Maybe. . . . Maybe."

"Why didn't you go home?"

"I was exhausted. I lay down here like a dog and slept, just for a few hours." He squinted around. "Or was that yesterday? What day is it?"

"It's Matthew's birthday," Robert said.

His uncle nodded. "It felt like one of those kinds of days. No one's playing pool, you know. I went into the hall. Parsons was asleep at the till. All the players were snoring on the floor." He rubbed his eyes again. Robert wanted to tell him to wash his hands before doing that. "I wish I could be a kid again, Robert. Everything was so much easier then. And better. As you get older, things get harder."

Harder? But things seemed hard now, Robert thought.

The mournful whistle of a train echoed through the town. It spoke of other lands, where lotus flowers unfurled the scent of sleep. Where the sun was warm and gentle and time moved as slowly as sap.

His uncle's eyelids had drooped. "So tired. I'll give you a ride home." He paused, wiped spittle from his lips. "Oh, right, I don't have my truck. Don't have any gas. I walked. Just gonna close my eyes. Don't go away, Robert. You have to tell me about *Twenty Thousand Leagues Under . . .*" Then he was asleep.

The train whistled again, the dreamy bass undertone rippling through the air. Robert forced his eyes to stay open. From the bench he had a clear view of the train station.

The engine was a dusky monster coming in from the east, the cowcatcher a metal smile. The train slowed to a stop, hissing steam, wheels sliding against the steel tracks. There were only three cars. No engineer. No one waited for the train's arrival.

Steam rolled out in vast clouds; the hissing grew quiet. Then there was a new hum that grew louder. Abram's truck rattled down the approach to the railway station and backed onto the loading platform.

Robert nudged his uncle and was rewarded with a soft snore.

He elbowed him again, and his head slipped heavily to the side. His uncle had stood for what was right. It had taken all his energy, but he hadn't signed his name.

Abram strode up to the engine, and three swarthy men lumbered out. They slid aside a door on the middle car and began loading something into Abram's truck. Robert couldn't see exactly what they were moving; it looked like metal wheels or gears. They seemed to be incredibly heavy.

If Abram was here, no one was at the rainmill. Maybe, Robert thought, I should sneak away. It's only a mile. I could look around. Just peek, really. And leave before Abram gets home again.

# CHAPTER TWENTY-TWO

ROBERT RAN TO THE EDGE OF TOWN, HOPPED ACROSS THE TRACKS, and kept running as fast as he could. After what seemed like hours, he glanced over his shoulder. Abram's truck was tiny now, and three toy-sized men continued to load it. Robert dashed over the grid road and into the fields, pushing through brambles, his feet slipping on the grass.

He felt older with each step. Ancient. He thought of the Greek messengers who used to run barefoot, bringing news of victory or defeat. One messenger had raced so hard and long his heart had burst. It had to do with a battle for Marathon against the Persian army.

He climbed a drainage ditch thick with weeds and flowers, grabbed on to the slick, leafy plants, and pulled himself over the edge. An image of his uncle Edmund flashed through his mind. Going over the trenches.

And getting a bullet in his heart.

Robert shuddered. Edmund had been at Horshoe today, in a reflection. Was maybe somehow watching right now. Edmund wouldn't have hesitated when he went over the trench, knowing there was something bad on the other side.

Robert knew he had to *do* something, finally. By summer it

would be too late. The rain would have washed everything from his mind. He would have crossed the cusp. He ran harder, his boots sinking deep into the soil and growing heavy with mud.

Finally, he caught sight of the rainmill: large and majestic, the vanes poised on the edge of motion, the bricks glistening. Beyond it the land was flat, the sky a blue dome. Robert didn't want to stare too long; he might lose his resolve.

Several yards later he stopped and scanned the farm. No sign or sound of Abram's truck. Robert padded up to the house and peeked in the front window. Gray shadows fell across the table; the room was empty. He crept around the corner. There, parked next to a fallen pig barn, was the RCMP car.

He couldn't see anyone inside it, but he ran over and opened the door anyway, hoping to find Sergeant Ramsden. The front seat was empty. Not even his Stetson was inside. Robert backed away, glanced around. The farmyard was still. He couldn't think of where to look. Was the sergeant even here? He might have ridden into town with Abram, just talking away about adult things. Fooled by Abram's fancy words.

Robert gulped some air. He'd have to go inside the house, where Abram kept all his secrets. Maybe he'd find a clue that would lead to Matthew.

Robert climbed the steps to the front door, found the courage to turn the knob, and pushed. The hinges creaked, but the door swung easily. A rotten-meat smell escaped, the stench ugly in his nostrils. He breathed through his mouth and sneaked into the front room.

The kitchen was clean, the table bare. One of the cupboard doors sat open. No plates. No bowls. It was as though Abram didn't eat at all.

The table reminded Robert that his mother would wonder why he hadn't come home for lunch. Maybe his parents were searching the fields for him right now and would get here in time to help find Matthew. Or were they sitting at their table, talking about the rain, the crops, and the rainmill, both of their sons forgotten?

He inched down the hall and pushed on a door. Inside was a flat bed of wooden slabs; no mattress, no blankets, not even a pillow. The sight of it disturbed him. Didn't Abram eat or sleep?

Robert knew exactly where to look next: the butterfly room. He was sure which room it was—the one facing east. It seemed like only yesterday he'd stood outside it and stared in.

He slid the bolt to one side and gently opened the door a crack. A moist, rotten crab-apple stink drifted out. He peered in. The thick vines had climbed to the ceiling, delved into every corner of the rafters with their feelers, and now hung down, brown and dripping with slime. Nothing was flying around inside.

He opened the door and slipped in. All the vines were dead. This room, once green and burgeoning, was a wasteland. The butterflies were gone. Not a sign of a lost wing or anything to indicate they'd ever been there.

Robert's feet stuck to the sludge, and he stepped through it carefully. He stood below the round window; the sun's light was dimmed by a brownish ooze that coated the pane. He gingerly parted some of the sticky vines, looking for the butterflies. There was nothing but a wall underneath, its paint peeling, the wood rotting.

Then a rustle—a whispering of wings and a lilting song, so light and familiar.

He turned slowly, as though he were caught in molasses. He knew, as sure as anything, who he would see, even before his eyes fell on her glowing blue shape.

Kachina.

She floated between him and the door. Alive. Beautiful. Graceful wings stroking the air. Her song was in his head, his bones. A melody that called him away from the world, urged him to follow her to a mystical place where he would sleep in peace.

She was so perfect. Her singing so gentle.

His eyelids grew heavy, slid closed. Peace. That was what he wanted. And sleep. No more fear.

Time passed slowly. He breathed deeply; the air was scented with flowers. A breeze caressed his cheeks. He opened his eyes and she fluttered closer. Her black, all-knowing orbs reflected star-like lights. There was a universe of harmony and warmth inside her.

He let his eyelids slide closed. No sadness. No pain. No worry.

*Worry.* The word stuck in his mind. *Responsibility.* Another word that grew heavier. I have a responsibility, he thought, a duty.

He opened his eyes. Kachina was only a few inches away, her singing insistent, higher in pitch. Her eyes were so close now that he saw he'd been mistaken about them: They were black insect eyes, barely able to reflect the light. They held nothing. No compassion. No wisdom.

She was Abram's tool. She had led the children away. There was nothing beautiful about that.

"I have a duty," he said plainly, reaching out. She flapped her wings as he tried to grasp her body. But he found nothing of substance. Instead, the touch of his hand made her singing grow sharper and she began to fall apart. She shed her color, the bright, hypnotic blue breaking off and twirling down, disappearing before it hit the ground. Tattered shreds of yellow and green burst out of her like tiny fireworks, until only a black husk remained, floating before him. Then, with a tiny, shrill noise, she flashed bright as the sun, folded in on herself, and was gone.

Robert blinked and lowered his hands. His fingers tingled. His eyes felt as though they'd been burnt by a flashbulb. He stumbled out of the room, rubbing his eyelids. With a shaking hand he closed the door, Kachina's final moments still blazing in his mind's eye.

He stood unsteadily in the hallway. He wasn't even sure exactly what had happened. His hands were numb and coated with a bluish, oily dust, which he wiped on his pants.

It seemed as though hours had passed, but light still brightened the kitchen window. No sound of Abram's truck. It was so loud he was sure he would hear it from miles away. He was running out of time, though, and there was still one more room to explore.

He went to the end of the hall and pushed open the door. He felt a chill, as though he were at the entrance to a mausoleum full of cold cemetery air. There was no window and his eyes didn't appear to be adjusting to the near darkness. A band of light revealed a table in the center of the room dominated by a glowing glass globe—a crystal ball. The rest of the room was dark. He gathered his courage and went inside, feeling colder with each step.

Jars were stacked on the floor. They looked like the broken one he'd found the day they discovered Matthew's hat. Robert touched the edge of one. It was smooth and cold. Pink dust stained his fingers.

The scent of roses wafted up and an image entered his head. He saw a girl running through a pasture, laughing, her pigtails flopping against her back. She had blond hair. *You can't catch me, na na na,* she sang. It was spring.

The vision disappeared. It wasn't a memory; he'd never seen the girl before. But the picture was so vivid.

He examined the dust on his hands. It was like the dust on the wings of butterflies. Was this what Abram collected? Robert pawed inside the jar, but there wasn't any more. Nor did he find some in the other jars.

On the table he discovered two old books, their black covers in tatters. An unlit candle in a brass holder sat next to a neatly laid-out collection of tiny doctor's instruments: scalpels, razor-sharp scrapers, and forceps with thin handles.

Robert lifted a scalpel. It was as light as air. He brushed the side of the blade, and the image of a boy playing in a bed of flowers appeared in his head, then vanished. He looked at his finger. Dust.

He dropped the scalpel. Abram had said there was a way to gather the dust—the stuff that surrounded people. Robert thought of Matthew and the other missing kids. All of them gathered and . . . and harvested.

His guts clenched, as though he were about to throw up. There was too much to understand. Too much to fear. He couldn't make sense of it.

A bursting light drew his attention to the crystal ball. A shooting star was falling through it. It faded out; then another appeared, and another. He edged nearer. Glowing sparks drifted behind the glass like a universe unfolding. He'd never seen such a display of light and beauty. His eyes moved back and forth, trying to follow each tiny firework. They were forming something, a shape. Like a flower. Or wings.

He had to touch it. Maybe then he'd reach right through the glass and feel the energy inside. He slowly extended his right arm, fingers trembling. The moment he pressed his fingertips against the ball, he felt a shock, but he couldn't pull his hand away. Without planning to, almost as if it weren't his intention at all, he laid his left hand on the globe.

The winged shape vanished. The ball grew dark and empty, filled with black forever. It was cold now, as though it had been carved from ice. He felt he might be sucked right into it.

*Why are you contacting us again?* A chorus of voices invaded his head, somber and otherworldly, coming out of the globe, from some far, far place where it was frigid and bleak. Where the locusts were large. *We are ready to deal. We are on our way. Why do you disturb our thoughts?*

He tried to pull his hands away, but they were frozen.

*The offerings are secured, are they not? Why so silent? Do not test our patience.*

Tendrils of thought were coming out of the globe, probing him. He had a vision of dark insect eyes. Of misshapen mouths and mandibles opening and closing.

Robert yanked his hands back and the ball clouded over. The voices still echoed in his mind. Their anger. Their malevolence. Their power.

Abram had sent a message to the stars. Robert had no doubt that these were the voices of the traders, and he never wanted to hear them again. He stumbled from the table, turned to leave, but stopped short.

A man was hiding behind the half-open door, had perhaps been there all along. He floated a few inches from the floor.

# CHAPTER TWENTY-THREE

**R**OBERT REMAINED STILL, BREATHING THROUGH HIS MOUTH. HE TOOK a step, but the man didn't move. A second step. Robert's heart thudded like a drum. He was ready to flee if the man so much as flicked his fingers.

Then he saw the Stetson on the floor, the yellow stripe on the man's pant leg.

"Sergeant Ramsden!" Robert edged closer. The sergeant's feet weren't touching the hardwood. His eyes stared straight ahead. "It's me, Robert Steelgate." He reached out and touched Ramsden's arm. No reaction.

He tugged the sergeant's sleeve, and Ramsden tumbled toward him, landing with a wet thud on the floor and striking the side of his face. He'd been hanging on a hook. Robert felt his neck; it was cold. No sign of a beating heart.

Then a slight pulse—blood moving in the veins. There it was again, seconds later. Ramsden's heartbeat was so slow it was as if he were hibernating. His chest rose and fell in tiny movements.

The sergeant's .455 Colt was still in its holster. There was no evidence of a struggle. Robert lifted the Mountie's arm and dropped it. "Wake up, Sergeant. Wake up!" He grabbed Ramsden's lapels.

"This is a special command. I *order* you to wake up, Sergeant Ramsden!"

Nothing. Not even a twitch.

Then the rumbling of Abram's truck sounded in the driveway, loud enough to rattle the crystal globe and the doctor's instruments. Robert shook the sergeant furiously but failed to wake him.

Robert ran to the front room and looked out the window. The truck was backed into the rainmill. Abram easily carried what looked to be a metal gear about the size of a tire into the mill, then returned for a second and a third. He spent a few minutes working out of sight. A bright light flashed inside.

Slowly the vanes turned and gradually gathered speed. Robert watched, fascinated. Soon they were whirring like a propeller. Already a cloud had appeared on the horizon, dark as the eyes of a grasshopper. The air hummed.

The butterflies were gone, so Abram had to be finished gathering dust and sending messages to the stars. Robert guessed he was bringing something other than rain this time. The traders. To barter for the souls of the children he had gathered.

Including Matthew.

Abram walked out of the rainmill and stood twenty feet away, watching. He'd taken off his hat, and the wind rustled his white hair. He turned toward the distant vortex of clouds unfurling from a hole in the sky. They were so black and vast they looked as though they were devouring the world.

Suddenly sparks shot out from an alcove halfway up the tower. One of the batteries exploded, showering the ground with glass. Abram watched the electrical display for a moment without reacting, then walked slowly to the small barn and stepped inside.

Robert slipped out the front door and ran toward the rainmill, his legs pumping hard, but the more he ran, the farther away the mill seemed. He stopped. He was in between the house and the tower, in the wide open. He ran again, this time harder, but he didn't get closer. Any moment now Abram would step out and spot him. Robert fixed his eyes on the mill; the tower seemed to be leaning over him. The thought of turning back flitted through his mind, but he ignored it. He closed his eyes and concentrated on moving his feet, the sound they made on the ground. It felt as if he was moving. He had to be.

He counted thirty steps, then opened his eyes again. He was under the shadow of the tower now and able to run. He dashed the last few feet, then stopped at the door on the far side and pulled. It was stuck. He looked behind him toward the barn and yanked again. The door flew open and he threw himself into the room at the heart of the rainmill, pulled the door shut, and banged the latch down.

He couldn't let Matthew go to that cold place hinted of in the crystal ball, be enslaved by the owners of those terrible voices.

The rainmill's interior buzzed and hummed with the warmth of a beehive. Gears spun above him; pulleys moved up and down;

electrodes ran here and there. At the center was the Mirror of All Things, laid flat. A pyramid of jars had been piled below it. A glowing light appeared along its surface.

Above it were the butterflies—eleven lights, each half the size of Kachina, gliding, ascending higher and higher. Blue. Violet. Red. Orange. Robert was drawn to them, his fear momentarily forgotten.

They were beautiful, their bodies glowing and transparent. Not real butterflies, he realized, but layers of sparkling dust that formed the same shape. They were trapped in a translucent bubble of energy.

He heard a sudden bang on the side of the rainmill. And another. He guessed Abram was taking a replacement battery up the ladder. The *ting ting* of a small metal hammer rang out. Thunder growled and roared through the sky as Abram worked. Maybe lightning will hit him, Robert thought. Judging by the sound, Robert figured Abram had to be at least three-quarters of the way up the tower. A big bolt of lightning would knock him right off.

There were several flashes, but no death cry or sound of a thudding body. Instead, the humming inside the rainmill doubled in intensity. Robert peeked out the tiny window in the door. The sun had vanished. Clouds surrounded the rainmill. Abram now stood in the open, hands on his hips, looking straight into the storm.

A section of the cloud unfolded and twirled to the ground. Abram didn't budge as it drew near to him. Shapes shifted inside the whirling fog, grew larger and more solid. Long, gaunt faces appeared and disappeared, glaring out with strange golden eyes and protruding, butterfly-like faces. The hairs on the back of Robert's neck rose. The traders were here.

A glowing butterfly appeared in the air. It zigged and zagged but was drawn toward the traders as though they were reeling in a kite. The butterfly fought to escape but was soon scooped up by an ebony hand, to disappear forever into the cloud. Robert's heart thudded. A soul had been harvested before his very eyes. The dealing had begun.

He looked back at the mirror. Now there were ten glowing lights hovering there. One shot up a glass tube that ran into the heights of the rainmill. Robert dashed over. If he could just get the butterflies out of the energy bubble.

The jars! That was what powered the mirror, just as they had the night at the theater. He grabbed at the top jar, then yanked his hand away. His skin was burnt, and a blister was already forming.

Only nine butterflies left.

A high-pitched metallic scream filled the room. The butterflies twirled faster. They darted back and forth as though panicking.

Robert found a loose brick, grabbed it tightly, and smashed a jar. Crimson light flashed, and the contents, a red glimmering dust, scattered across the floor.

He smashed a second jar and was rewarded with another flash, this time blue. Then he hit a third and a fourth, swinging crazily. He would never see his brother again. Tears ran down his face. He thought he heard Mike Tuppence's sad voice, screaming *Robert . . . Robert . . . Robert*. Then there were only eight lights. He was too slow!

He struck again and again, swinging with all his might, sweat on his brow. The room filled with the voices of children. Words flooded through his head. *Splendor. Glory. Strike now. Strike hard. Onward. Thermopylae. Vimy*. The dust spilled out of the jars; the glow in the mirror grew dim. All the jars were broken.

And still the butterflies were trapped inside the energy bubble. An emerald butterfly flew to the edge. Quite suddenly Robert felt a presence. A familiar, solemn presence.

"Matthew," he said, breathless. "Matthew, come home." He struck the Mirror of All Things—sparks flew from the glass. It was like hitting solid ice. He swung a second time. A crack formed, and blue light poured out. Robert swung again, and the mirror shattered into a thousand reflecting shards that sliced the air. A scream pierced the room, as if the mirror had been a living thing. The butterflies scattered.

"Get out of here!" he yelled. "Fly away!"

They fluttered against the walls, searching desperately for escape. Then one found a small window and slipped out. The rest followed.

Robert dropped the brick, his hands burning. With the butterflies gone, the mill had grown dark. Only the occasional explosion of sparking electricity in the walls above him lit his way. He stumbled toward the door.

It swung open. Abram stood there, the clouds swirling behind him. His hair was plastered against his forehead, he'd lost his dark glasses, and his red, red eyes glowed with anger.

"No!" he yelled hoarsely. "You little fool!"

Robert backed up to the pile of broken jars. Gears began to grind, as if the oil had dried up; the pulleys shrieked like banshees.

"You've destroyed years of work!"

Abram crossed the floor in a heartbeat, his right arm out, his hand jabbing into Robert's throat, squeezing like a claw. Robert tried to squirm free, but Abram's fingers dug deep into his windpipe, choking him.

He was going to die. He had rescued his brother, and no one would know about it. He would be nothing but a dead boy, buried in the sandhills.

Abram's face was a skull, hard and unforgiving. This was a man, Robert knew, who had led legions of Roman soldiers into Gaul. Had stood on the walls of Troy and taunted the Greeks. A general. A king. A hundred men had died at his hand. A thousand, maybe more. He had outlived them all.

And Robert, tiny Robert, had dared to stand up to him. Foolhardy, Robert thought, impertinent fool. There was no air left in his lungs. He saw nothing but gray.

Then the sooty clouds, which were drifting nearer, stole into the rainmill. A sulfuric, rancid stench followed. A black, impossibly long arm reached out of the clouds and grasped Abram's shoulder, making it disappear, as if erased.

*You called us. You must pay us.*

Abram turned his head, went rigid. "No," he spat. Another shadow hand grabbed him.

*A price. A price.*

*You must meet the price.*

Abram screamed and was yanked backward, letting Robert slip from his clutches.

Robert fell to the floor, scraping his cheek so hard that blood trickled down his face. He tried to suck in air but failed. His windpipe felt crushed. His vision swam with images. He managed to gulp a breath, then another, until his lungs were full. He squinted.

Abram was a few feet away, twisting around as though he were wrapped in a black shroud. He let out a gurgling, muffled yell and charged straight at Robert, every ounce of his will focused on escape. He nearly broke free, but willowy appendages, seemingly made of nothing more than smoke, clutched him tight and pulled him back.

The sulfur was so strong now that Robert's eyes burnt. But he couldn't look away. Parts of Abram were disappearing into the murk. A leg. An ear. A hand. His gurgling was cut off as his torso vanished. His eyes still blazed red, his brow furrowed, fighting to the last, glaring at Robert.

Robert didn't budge. He narrowed his eyes, finding the strength to glare back. A moment passed. Abram blinked, looked confused; then, with a soft, wispy rustle, the clouds enveloped him.

Robert pushed himself to his feet. Where Abram had stood there were only tendrils of thick fog. The shapes retracted into the leech-colored clouds and retreated out the door.

Robert stood, but his legs were so weak he was barely able to keep his feet. Abram was gone. Defeated. Taken to some other place, or destroyed. The traders had extracted their price.

Victory! Now he knew what soldiers felt at the end of a battle. The thought that he had won was beyond all imagining. It gave him strength. *So there!* he wanted to yell. *Take that!*

The rainmill's vanes ground to a halt. A moment of silence followed and Robert listened, his heart beating hard in his chest, his blood pounding in his ears. He'd stopped the mill! He'd done it.

A deep grumble sounded from the top of the mill. Robert squinted up into the darkness. Sparks of light were shooting out of the heights, arcing down toward him like falling stars, burning out before they hit the ground. He could make a wish on each one. A thousand wishes. Another barrage of sparks cascaded down. It looked beautiful. Like fireworks. His pupils dilated when a bright hissing flash lit the whole inside of the mill from top to bottom. He'd caused this. Made it happen.

The rumbling returned. Then the bricks rattled and the ground began to shake. Metal bars groaned, and a brick *thunk*ed down next to him, making him jump.

He ran for the door, thinking how stupid he'd been to stand there staring into space, gloating. The door seemed so far away, and everything was shaking now. A thin bar struck his shoulder hard, and he staggered, nearly falling. A beam crashed across his path. He leapt over it but caught his foot and fell, scraping his hand. He scrambled upward, half crawling, half running out the door, not stopping until he was a hundred yards away.

He turned to see the mill shudder, as if it were trying to take a step. It wobbled back and forth, the top leaning to one side. A glass battery exploded with a popping sound. Then the tower imploded, bricks bursting apart as they hit the ground. Within seconds, the mill was a heap of broken bits and protruding steel joists. Only the occasional spark appeared.

The clouds were distant now, withdrawing into a hole in the sky. The traders were leaving, back to whatever realm they had come from.

Seven glowing butterflies winged through the air, circling Robert.

# CHAPTER TWENTY-FOUR

Robert was dazzled.

They alighted in his hair, landed on his shoulders, drawn to him as though he were a magnet. Tinkling voices echoed, so softly he couldn't make out the words. He could only sense feelings of warmth. Relief. Thankfulness.

"You're safe," he said, not sure if he believed it himself. "You're safe."

He held out his hand and the emerald creature perched in his palm, wings folding and unfolding.

*Thank you, Robert,* he heard Matthew say, *for helping us.*

Robert's lip trembled, his eyes watered, but now was not the time for tears. The butterflies were so fragile that a strong gust of wind might tear them apart. He had to get them all away from here so nothing bad could ever happen to them again.

"Follow me," he said, lowering his hand and allowing Matthew to take to the air.

Robert jogged back to Abram's house, the butterflies trailing behind him like ribbons on a kite. The dark clouds were gone, and the sun was shining brightly again. It felt as if a whole week had gone by in the past few hours. He opened the door and scrunched up his nose. The smell of rot was worse than before. The floorboards creaked beneath his feet as he made his way cautiously to the back room.

The butterflies grew agitated. They flew to the far corner and swooped down at the floor and into the air, moving like a tiny Ferris wheel.

"What's wrong?" he asked. It was too dark for him to see the other side of the room. The only light, coming from the slight glow of the butterflies, revealed a hint of floorboards. And something else—a glinting handle.

He grabbed the candle from the table but couldn't find matches. He squinted around the room.

Sergeant Ramsden was still lying in the same position. Robert knelt beside him. The Mountie's chest rose and fell; his face was slack with sleep. Robert squeezed his arm, lifted an eyelid, but got no response. He wondered what would happen if none of the adults woke up. The thought chilled him.

A Mountie would have matches: Mounties were prepared for every emergency. He patted Ramsden's front pockets. Empty. He briefly touched the holster, the grip of the revolver. Beside it was a small leather pouch. Robert flipped it open, dug inside, and pulled out a pair of tweezers, a small jackknife, and at the bottom, a metal tube. He opened it and discovered three wooden matches.

He quickly struck one against the rough side of the tube. A flame sparked to life. He lit the candle and strode to the far side of the room.

There, outlined in the floor, was a trapdoor.

# CHAPTER TWENTY-FIVE

**R**OBERT SET THE CANDLE DOWN. THE GLOWING BUTTERFLIES WERE zooming so fast that they had become nothing more than colored streaks. He grabbed the metal ring and pulled. It was like hefting a stone from an Egyptian tomb. He strained every muscle, relying on his legs to lift the weight.

The door rose an inch. Two inches. The flickering light revealed that the door had been cut from a slab of stone, with wooden floorboards fastened to the top.

Robert was afraid he'd never have enough strength. But if he let go now, he wouldn't be able to lift it again. He pulled harder, thinking of all the work he'd done that summer and how it must have made him stronger. A grating sound echoed in the room. He'd managed to open the door another few inches.

Not enough. Then, with a flash of emerald and crimson light, the butterflies surrounded him, filling him with a sense of his own power. For a moment he felt he could do anything. With a final effort he heaved, grunting aloud. The door swung over and slammed into the floor.

The butterflies dove into the black hole, winging down into darkness. A chill escaped the room below. Abram had carved this cave under the prairie—just standing on the edge of it made Robert nervous. Maybe it was Abram's final trap.

Robert picked up the candle and carefully descended a set of stone steps. His flesh shook; his teeth chattered. The coldest winds of winter lived here.

He held the light above his head. The room was circular, and crammed with statues of children, an arctic mist curling at their feet. The butterflies darted from statue to statue, avoiding long, thin icicles that hung from the roof. There were at least twenty figures, all facing north, mouths open as though they were singing an anthem.

He examined one. It was too perfect to be a statue; too real. An unfamiliar boy, maybe six years old, was wrapped in a frosty sheet that blurred his features. His eyes were wide open, as though he'd just seen a remarkable sight. He was wearing loose, silky clothes from another country. He looked Arabian.

Beside him was a girl with pigtails who could have been frozen on her way to a picnic. An icy film clung to her summer dress. Her eyes too were filled with wonder.

Robert crossed his arms, trying to keep warm. He gritted his teeth. These were kids. Just kids. They were supposed to be out playing, eating cookies, or going to school. Not frozen here.

Then there was a *crack!* One of the butterflies had flown directly into the forehead of a statue. The ice around it shattered and the figure wobbled for a moment, then collapsed.

Robert couldn't believe his eyes. He stood there agog, not sure what to do.

Then, as another butterfly landed on a girl's head, a second *crack!*

*Crack! Crack! Crack!* Robert sucked in a breath. Three more children, free of their icy encasements, fell over. One of these could be Matthew, he thought.

He rushed to a fallen form. It was a young girl. The ice was gone, and steam rose from her body. She lay curled up like a baby. Her eyes were closed tight. Robert touched her. "Wake up, it's time to go home," he whispered. The girl's skin was ice cold. He held the candle closer. It was Susan Vaganski, wearing the same clothes she'd had on when Robert had last seen her, on the way home from school.

She was breathing. Alive!

A flicker of green caught his attention. An emerald butterfly was resting on top of a small boy, sinking into the ice that coated him.

*Crack!* The ice splintered around him, tinkling as it fell. It was Matthew! He stood still for a moment, and gasped as though he'd been underwater; then his knees gave out and he fell. Robert tried to catch him but was too late. He turned his brother over and pulled him onto his lap. Matthew's eyes were shut tight, but he was breathing, his face still sheathed in ice.

"Matthew, wake up, we can go home now." Robert touched his brother's cheek. "I didn't forget you. I never will. I mean it."

He lifted Matthew, finding him light as straw, carried him up the stairs, and gently laid him on the floor near Sergeant Ramsden.

He paused to gently smooth his brother's hair, then returned to the cave.

Six more sleeping children were ready to go home. One by one, Robert took them in his arms and brought them upstairs, placing them next to his brother.

Robert caught his breath, then made a final trip down. The rest of the children were still statues. He walked from frozen boy to frozen girl, resisting the impulse to count. He didn't want to know the number lost.

He found Mike Tuppence rigid with frost. He was wearing his suspenders, ragged pants, and an old shirt, and he had no shoes on. His eyes were two marbles. Robert touched his classmate's lifeless face. Mike had been a friend of Matthew's. Now he was dead. Robert backed away.

When he was sure no one else could be saved, Robert wearily climbed back up the steps. The children were still lying where he'd left them. He glanced at the table. The crystal ball was dim; with only the light from the hall to give it its glow, it reflected Robert back to himself. He wondered if he should break it. Or would that unleash something ugly? What if it called the traders back?

But he couldn't leave it. Maybe someone like Abram would discover it. Or worse, maybe Abram would find his way back through it. The thought made Robert shudder.

He lifted one of the larger metal pokers from the table. He

had to strike before he lost his nerve. The ball might explode and kill him, but it had to be destroyed. He squeezed his eyes shut and swung. *Thud.* He'd missed. He squeezed again, swung. *Thud.* But he was sure he'd had it lined up—it was as though it had moved.

He swung a third time, eyes open. *Crash!* The ball broke, and shards of glass flew across the tabletop. There was no explosion, no sudden vacuum of blackness sucking him in. In fact, it sounded like little more than a bowl breaking.

"Whazzat?" the sergeant murmured, rolling onto his side and blinking. He looked up at Robert. "What was that?"

"I just broke something," Robert said. "That's all."

The sergeant got to his knees and gawked at the seven children. "Who are these kids?"

"The ones Abram stole. I found them in the cellar." Robert pointed. "There's Matthew and Susan Vaganski. I don't know who the others are." He was surprised that he had to explain this to Ramsden. The sergeant should have known who these kids were and where they'd come from. It was his job. "There were more. But they're . . ." Robert couldn't find the right word.

Ramsden stood, dazed. Then he shook his head and grimaced. Robert knew he was summoning up his will, becoming a man of action. It was part of his training. Ramsden walked over to one of the children. The girl lifted a hand toward him and he took it in his huge paws. "They're freezing."

"They were encased in ice."

The sergeant looked up, narrowed his eyes. "Where's Abram?"

"Dead, I think." Robert swallowed, wondered how he would ever explain the traders and butterfly-shaped souls. Ramsden was past the cusp. It would be better to make something up for now. "The tower fell down. Abram was inside it."

"I have to see that for myself, once these kids have been looked after," Ramsden said, lifting the girl into his arms. "They're so cold. I don't know how they can still be alive. We should—"

"Move them into the sun," Robert finished. He was already leaning over and picking up Matthew. "That's what they need."

He carried Matthew out into the open. He was still cold, but the hot sun would soon warm him to the bone.

Robert opened the passenger door of the RCMP car and laid his brother gently on the seat. Matthew twitched; his eyes opened. He stared up at Robert with frightened, unblinking eyes.

"I went walking," Matthew said slowly. "I went walking and this man picked me up. We drove right by Horshoe."

"Don't worry," Robert whispered, "everything's all right now. Don't think about it anymore." He squeezed his brother's hand. "Soon you'll be home, all tucked in your bed. Mom'll heat the water bottle up for you, take the chill off."

Ramsden joined them, cradling a red-haired girl who looked like a doll in his arms.

"They're in shock," Ramsden said, opening the back door.

"They've been asleep for a long time," Robert explained.

He and the sergeant carried all seven children out of the house. It was good to see them safe in the car, huddled tightly together. Ramsden stared at the wreckage of the rainmill, shaking his head as though he were trying to rid himself of a bad dream. He opened his mouth, then shut it.

"I've got to see what's in that cellar," he said, and he marched back into Abram's house.

Robert got into the front seat and pulled Matthew onto his lap. His brother was warming up. Robert used his shirtsleeve to dry droplets of water from Matthew's cheek. It was wonderful to see his face. He tried to memorize it so he'd never forget again.

When Sergeant Ramsden returned, he was pale. Getting in behind the wheel, he said, "It's terrible. It's the worst thing I've ever seen."

Robert nodded, knowing it was even worse than Ramsden realized—for those kids, their souls were gone, snuffed out like candles.

"We'd better get them all home," Ramsden said. "Then I have phone calls to make. Work to do."

Soon the road blurred by as the car bumped along. Robert held Matthew tight. Susan Vaganski sat beside him, her head on his shoulder. There was another girl next to her. The other four were in the back, scrunched together. Some slept. Others hid their eyes from the light. One boy was crying, murmuring in another language.

The sun had declared war on the green fields. Robert felt its angry heat through the windshield, bringing out the sweat, ridding him of the chill from the cellar. He put his hand up to the window to block the light, then lowered it. Better to let it shine.

They turned toward Horshoe, rolling down the access road, passing under the shadow of the grain elevators. The streets were empty. A breeze scattered several papers across the road. The town looked deserted to Robert, as though everyone were playing hide-and-seek and he was the seeker.

Ramsden turned the corner onto Main Street and Robert was surprised to see that a crowd had gathered, maybe twenty people. Mr. Ruggles was in the middle of the street, staring left and right. Ramsden steered around him and Ruggles gawked into the car. He looked confused. Other townspeople were gaping at the sky, rubbing their heads. Mrs. Juskin was there, clutching her pointer as though she were about to teach a lesson. They passed the laundry; the Chinese looked directly at Robert, no emotion on their faces. Then one nodded.

Ramsden pulled the car up in front of the hotel. He and Robert got out. People stepped back a bit from them. Some stared at Robert; others looked at the ground, sneaking sheepish glances up at him. They know, Robert thought. They're waking up from their dreams and they know that everything has changed.

He turned back to help Susan Vaganski. She stood, wobbly, then stumbled ahead. Her father caught her in a bear hug; her plump mother embraced them both. Mr. Vaganski stroked Susan's hair and whispered, "Thanks," in Robert's direction.

Then a man moaned sadly beside them and fell to his knees. It was Mr. Tuppence, Mike's father. Mrs. Juskin comforted him, saying, "There, there." Robert swallowed. If only there had been a way to bring Michael Tuppence back.

Uncle Alden pushed through the crowd. He'd splashed water on his face; he looked wide-eyed. He glanced into the car, and when he saw Matthew, he leaned in and touched his cheek. Shaking his head, Uncle Alden looked down at Robert and said, "Somehow, you did it. Didn't you?"

Robert nodded, feeling the weight of his uncle's hand on his shoulder.

"I . . . I . . ." Uncle Alden stumbled, his words slow. "I'm proud of you."

Robert gave him a hug; then he and Ramsden got back into the car with the rest of the kids. Robert waved to his uncle as they putted down the street. Once on the main road, Ramsden sped up.

How many times have I been down this road? Robert wondered, and then he realized he sounded like an old person. He was young. He shouldn't be counting things like that yet.

Sergeant Ramsden pulled up to Robert's house as the sun was touching the horizon, turning the windows red and bright. "Tomorrow," he said slowly, as though every word was an effort, "we'll have a long talk."

"We will," Robert agreed.

Ramsden got out and opened the passenger door. Robert scooped up Matthew and carried him toward the house. Hearing Ramsden's footsteps behind him, he turned and said, "Thanks, Sergeant, I can handle it from here." He was surprised at how deep his voice was.

The sergeant smiled, saluted Robert, and got into the car. Robert watched as he drove away.

Still clutching Matthew, Robert opened the door to his home. The scent of beef and boiled cabbage flooded the house. Maybe they were going to have cabbage rolls, Robert thought. It was exactly what he needed. His stomach felt as empty as a galleon.

His mother stood at the stove; his father sat at the table. They looked up at him as he walked in with Matthew. Both froze, staring and silent, as though they were looking at an apparition. His father swallowed, his Adam's apple moving slowly under his skin. "You brought him home," he whispered. "I'd given up hope."

"I remembered him," Robert said simply.

His mother took an uncertain step. Her lips were parted; she was trying to speak but couldn't as tears slid down her cheeks. "I didn't . . . I didn't . . . dear God," she whispered finally.

Robert said nothing. There were no words to describe what he felt. He lowered Matthew to the floor and helped him stand.

Matthew smiled, lifted a small hand. His parents rushed to him, his mother hugging and kissing him, sobbing all the while, his father wrapping his arms around the whole family, drawing them together. His parents began to weep, the way people did in the Bible, big tears rolling down their cheeks.

Robert felt as if he were holding them all up. He stood there for a long time, and at one point he was sure he heard his mother whisper, "I love you. I will always love you." And later she said, directly into Robert's ear, "Thank you for finding him; for bringing him home."

# CHAPTER TWENTY-SIX

THE SUN SHONE STRONG THE NEXT DAY, BURNING AWAY THE MOISture, drying up the grass. The ground hardened. A hot, sucking wind swooshed out of the sky, followed by a storm of locusts.

In his room, Robert looked out the window. The tumbleweeds were tumbling. The world was as it should be.

Dishes clinked downstairs. Put them upside down, Mom, he thought. Soon she'd be complaining about the gritty taste of dust in her coffee. Or the gravy. It wouldn't be there forever; the drought would end someday, Robert was sure of that.

Matthew was curled up in his bed, sleeping soundly, the blankets sculpted around him. Robert's mom and dad had been up to the room three times already to see if he was awake. Each time they had crept back down, whispering, "Let him sleep."

Robert was full of joy. Matthew was back. And yet, it wasn't perfect. He couldn't help thinking of all those empty beds in other houses. Homes with one less child. All gone because of Abram.

I did what I could, he thought. There was consolation in that.

The night before, Uncle Alden had come by to be with them. He had given Robert a long hug and handed him a thick book called *The History of the World.* It was as though he were bestowing a prize. Robert's parents had thanked Uncle Alden, saying it was a very thoughtful gift, because Robert should be reading and learning more. Then, as if to prove their point, they had talked about the price of wheat, of beef, about the government, and about taxes. At bedtime, his father had silently shaken his hand, his way of saying thanks. Robert might never be able to explain to them what had happened; he could barely explain it to himself.

He just wanted to forget everything today. Start new. He didn't even want to read. It might be a while before he picked up the Jules Verne book again.

He had his brother now. His family. Everything would be all right. He gazed out his window at the Cypress Hills and the mysterious blue-tinged sky.

Going on and on forever.

# ABOUT THE AUTHOR

Arthur Slade was born in Moose Jaw, raised on a ranch in the Cypress Hills, and educated at the University of Saskatchewan. He now writes full-time from Saskatoon, Saskatchewan, Canada. He is the author of six novels for young adults and has won several prizes, including the Governor General's Award for Children's Literature. Arthur Slade can be visited virtually at www.arthurslade.com.